Fish Tails & Lady Legs

Dear Susan,
    May your song
and your passion continue
guiding you forward.
                ♡ Pascale

and happy birthday!

Fish Tails & Lady Legs

AN EROTIC NOVEL

Pascale Kavanagh

For my own little mermaid, whose song changed everything.

CONTENTS

1
UNDERWATER

She let out a deep sigh, the bubble containing her would-be sound floating all the way up to the surface, untouched. There it lingered for just a moment before popping softly, heard by no one. There were numerous sounds deep in the ocean, but none of that variety. A sigh was not a productive issuance from a mermaid and so dissolved into nothing.

It was another day in the cold, dark ocean for Lalune. Another day yearning for anything outside her watery home.

"Lalune! Where are you?" She could hear her sisters calling for her. Or more accurately, she could feel the vibration of the sound. She supposed it was time enough to get started with the day. Floating around wasn't going to grow her legs any faster.

Lalune was partially glad to have her reveries interrupted. Pondering the hopelessness of her life did not make for a wonderful start of the day. There was plenty to do to keep busy in the vast ocean, and many creatures to keep her occupied and even entertained. Maybe a bit of distraction would be helpful.

"Lalune, why are you always hiding out in Nori Cove? Do you have treasure back there? I just can't imagine what could be so interesting??!"

"I like to have a little private time, for my thoughts. Is that so bad? I'm not hiding anything, I promise." Did anyone believe her? Did she believe herself?

"That sounds terribly boring, sister. And it makes you morose. Who's ever heard of a sad mermaid?? It's just not natural. We are the most beautiful and interesting creatures on the planet. What is there to be sad about?"

"I'm not sad, necessarily. I just like to think about things. And I think all of the world's creatures are beautiful and interesting. Even... the land-walkers." She knew this statement would not be taken well, but said it anyway.

"Ughhh. They are just awful! Clumsy, rude, unkind. Haven't you seen how they act? Thank goodness they could never be in our world. And I would never want to go out there. Especially since everything is perfect down here."

Lalune nodded, pretending she agreed. In her heart, that was the furthest from the truth. Most mermaids had nothing but disdain for the land-walkers, but Lalune felt differently. In her eyes, they were splendid.

Not that she knew this from any personal experience. The stories she heard from her friends and family were amplified to grand proportions by her own imagination. An entire fantasy lived in her head, about their charmed lives, and the wide variety of experiences they must be having. The one that was most intriguing, of course, was their ability to make music. She could hear it sometimes, all the way from the distant shore, vibrating through the water. It was mesmerizing.

Many of the creatures in her world could make music – she especially loved the whales' song – but it was not the same. There was a sense of joy in the land-walker's music, not just utility. The land-walkers made music for the sheer pleasure of it, not just for basic communication. Lalune knew this had to be true based on how the sounds she heard made her feel.

Fish Tails & Lady Legs

Despite all the others thinking it was reckless and ridiculous, because only land-walkers sing and sea creatures hum, Lalune loved to sing. The pleasure of hearing her sound, carried on the soft breeze above her home, made her feel alive. Yet her song was stifled and muted in the sea, where she was supposed to keep herself hidden. She knew that on land it could be heard in its fullness, from the few times she had snuck over to the island and let herself sing. She knew, without knowing why or how, that it would be on land that her voice, and her life, would find its purpose. Each day, it became more and more difficult to stay silent in the depths.

Lalune had known since she was a child that she had been built for something different than the life she was living, if only she could figure out how to get it. What she wanted most in the world, enough to give up everything she currently knew, was to be a land-walker. To have two beautiful legs that would carry her around on the land, and to hear her song, her true voice, carried through the air. This would be her salvation.

Still, the ocean contained everything she knew. Why couldn't she be satisfied with that life? Why did she come to believe that her only hope was to leave everything behind? No one else seemed to suffer this same malady, this discontent. Her friends and family were perfectly happy with their magical kingdom.

A large tail flapping in front of her once again startled her out of her daydreams. Her sisters had swum away and she was supposed to be following them.

Off she went to live another day in the life of a magical mermaid. There were adornments to create, games to play, and beautiful scenes to explore. She and her sisters were close (other than the big secret Lalune carried) and had a vast repertoire of diversions to keep them occupied. Occasionally they would sneak up towards the surface and watch the land-walkers fumble around in the water. It caused no shortage of giggles, except from Lalune, who observed with awe.

She could see herself, wiggling those legs and needing that funny facemask to breathe. All their awkwardness was endearing, and she could only imagine how poorly she would do in their environment. It would be impossible, actually.

She wanted to know the feeling of sand between her toes, sun on her skin and the beauty of her song in the faces of those who heard it. Could she find her boldness, her voice, and take her place in the other world?

The legends said it was possible to transform, to grow legs where her tail used to be, but what if it wasn't true? What if Lalune was destined to live out her days swallowing this secret, ashamed and unheard?

It was too easy to hide in the darkness, and nearly impossible to live with her desire. Without being able to sing freely, all the magic in the ocean was useless to her. Her beauty, her talent, even the love in her heart, were all wasted.

There was no one to talk to about this, and certainly no guides she could ask for help. The land-walkers knew of song, but not of mermaids, and the mermaids knew nothing of a two-legged life. It was a leap of faith, to believe all the pieces would come together, but what choice did she have?

Lalune's search for someone to guide her, someone who knew the way, had to be done in secrecy. No one could discover her desire to leave their underwater kingdom. There were severe consequences for mermaids who tried to cross over and did not succeed. Making it all the way through to the other side would be her only option.

What scared her most was knowing she could never come back. The comfort and familiarity of her dark depths, as unsatisfactory as they were, would be lost to her forever. She would live or die as a land-walker.

2
MONIQUE

"Mama!!!"

Is it wrong to wish that your children were mute?

"MAAAMAAAA!!!!"

Ok, maybe it would be easier if I was deaf.

"MAAAAAAAAMMMMAAAAAAAA!!!!!!!!!"

Somebody better be about to lose a limb over there, I think as I stomp over to the bedroom.

"Yes! What requires so much yelling?" I ask as I realize I am also yelling. They are startled by my testy response. I feel immediately guilty.

"Mama, Lola was doing a perfect handstand! She did it, she really did it! Oh my God, it was so amazing. She just balanced there like her hands were her feet. It was so cool..."

My sweet Claire is jumping up and down, just like her aunt Lizzy always does.

I look over at Lola, beaming. She has been working so hard to do this, and now can't even talk. She's happily accepting the accolades from her usually critical big sister.

"Let me see," I say with a smile I can't help.

The girls set themselves up near the wall and Claire positions herself as the spotter. She begins coaching her little sister, telling her when to breathe and how to adjust to keep the balance. She is encouraging and supportive.

I look at my baby girl, standing so powerfully upside down, not even using the wall for balance. I feel a tinge of jealousy, which I have to release as Lola comes smoothly down. Lola has an uncanny sense of her body, so graceful and strong, and so unlike the gangly, clumsy one I carry around. Except when I dance. Then my body expresses all the grace I imagine a woman should have.

"How did it look, Mama?"

I almost don't have the words.

"It was perfect, baby. You totally nailed it. Like a flagpole. I really liked how you held your arms really strongly and pointed your feet. Wow! I am completely impressed.

And you, Claire... what a great coach you are! I didn't know you could do that. You guys are incredible."

I wrap my arms around my girls. My strong, beautiful, talented girls. I am happy. And lucky. To be their mother and to have this life and to witness their greatness. I bury them with deep squeezes and slurpy kisses.

"Who's hungry?"

We all scramble to the kitchen so that I can finish making their dinner. This is our brand new life. It still feels awkward, even after more than a year, but I pray it will feel natural before too much longer. I have to get used to this new way of being. Like relearning how to ride a bike, the process is causing some soreness in tender places.

My knives are getting dull. I'm frustrated about the extra effort I have to put in to get through the carrots. I have gotten so lazy, after having been so fanatical for all those years. Everything is harder, now that I am out of practice. But the girls love it anyway. They don't complain that my vegetables aren't perfectly diced, or that my sauces are lumpy instead of silken.

This meal, however, is all delicious flavors and sweet little-girl giggles. With every smile and compliment from them, I remember how un-accommodating I had been to their calls just a short while before. And all they wanted was to celebrate with me. My companions of shame and inadequacy settle in to either side of my squeaky chair at the kitchen table.

I can't even claim that motherhood is new to me – Claire is 11 and Lola is about to turn 7 - but the learning curve just isn't letting up. Sometimes I revert to being the selfish little girl who has always been in the middle of all my siblings' needs, and just wants her own time and privacy. I don't want to share and I don't want to be responsible. Sometimes, all I want is to be invisible.

This little girl has grown up and is now somebody else's mother. For how much I adore my own girls, I can't seem to get past my own self-centeredness. What, I wonder, has made me so selfish and needy? Why can't I just be the person I want to be? I hardly allow the answer to fully form in my head.

My phone starts singing the pop song Claire installed as my ringtone. It's Nora, my older sister.

"What's up?" I ask, startled out of a potential spiral.

"Can you come over tomorrow night?"

"I guess… is something going on?"

"Nope." The answer is a bit sharp. "We just want to see you. I know it's been a shit-storm over there. Just come over, OK?"

I'm not really in the mood to hang out with my sisters. They'll want to talk about all the drama, and it's just too exhausting. I'd much rather avoid and deny, frankly.

But there's no getting out of this, I think. When Nora wants something, she gets it.

"Fine." I know I sound ungracious. "Thanks Nora. See you tomorrow."

Family. Mine is better than most, I have to admit, but we are an odd bunch with such diverse interests, strengths and personalities. Of my siblings, Nora, the oldest, was given an extra portion of brains, Danny got the best personality and Lizzy, the baby, got exuberance. My gift? A strange affinity to blades and flames, and the ability to create something from nearly nothing.

That skill served me well in the kitchen, but kept me constantly in the world of my imaginings. It made me a daydreamer, like our mother. It also allowed my hypersensitivity to blossom into fantastical stories that helped me easily escape the world, for better or worse. Family, however, was something I had yet to successfully escape.

Bedtime is easier than usual. The meal seems to have shifted us past my earlier grumpiness, and everyone is in a good mood. I don't allow the worry about going to my sister's tomorrow night to consume me, although I can feel it trying to make it's way to the front of my thoughts.

The girls and I fall into bed playful and snuggly, a tangle of little bodies and big bodies, all vying for the best patch of bed and the most comfortable corner of pillow. We don't do it as often anymore, but when we pile into my enormous bed, I have a glimpse into the feelings I used to have… that everything, in fact, is perfectly fine. The next thing I realize, we've all fallen asleep. As it's been for so many nights, sleep does not last.

I squint at the clock across the room. *Shit*, my eyesight seems to get worse by the day. *Does it say 2 or 3? Does it matter?* I'm awake. A few attempts at re-settling don't prove useful, so I undertake the task of untangling myself from my babies and heading downstairs to my little office. There's nothing so urgent that it needs my attention in the middle of the night, but still I feel it's important to use this rare stretch of peace and quiet fully. Might as well get some work done.

I can't shake the bad feeling about tomorrow. Sure, I've been avoiding my family since all hell broke loose in my life. Everyone else seems to be doing so well in their lives, and it's been one disaster after another for me. After such an illustrious start, too. Oh well, I know it's just temporary. At least I hope so.

I just don't want to get lectured. Or questioned. I know they disapprove of my career change, leaving my soul's calling. They want me to live the grand life I used to, the rising star chef whose life is all passion and glory. I don't know how to be that woman anymore and I just don't have the strength right now. My girls have to come first. My sisters just don't understand.

It's no secret that I had walked away from the only area in my life in which I had consistently felt successful. I was flying, then cut my own wings off to be with the other land-dwellers. Here, on the hard ground, I am hardly good for anything other than cooking, which I'm not doing any more. My relationships are pathetic, I am never satisfied with how much time or attention I give my girls, and the work of suppressing my primary creative outlet has left me tired and grumpy. But I can't see any other choice. At least for right now. I'm a single mom now – I need a paycheck and a career that does not have me out all night, every night.

The job at the magazine, I have to admit, has been a godsend. It not only pays the bills, but also lets me do something that's useful to the world. I can live in the inventions of my imagination, a place I land in quite often, and am happy enough to be writing. Sure, it isn't the same passion I feel for cooking, but it's good enough. It's the right choice for my family.

The bright lights of my screensaver remind me that the article about romantic meals in the city needs finishing. Having already done the research on restaurants offering the most unique Valentine's Day meals, all that remains is to include recipes for people to cook at home. Romantic meals are a part of my distant past, at this point, and I could just as easily be researching Mars.

I rarely let myself feel the depth of my loneliness, but it is always with me. It has been a string of failed attempts at love since my failed marriage. I have to be thankful that Jeff and I are now on good terms, but the road getting here nearly destroyed me.

All the stories – my divorce, the end of my career as a rising star in the restaurant world, the recent deaths of my brother and parents – stream before my eyes like a personalized movie from which I can't pull myself away.

So often, life, in all its dimensions, is too much for me to handle. It has been feeling like that quite often these days. When I slip into the stories in my head, or on the page, life is Goldilocks' version of *just right*. I become brave, kind and utterly capable. I stop betrayal in its tracks, and dish out a healthy dose of whatever's needed for any situation. My fantasies replace my relationships and my time in the kitchen. No need for lovers when the ones in my mind are always perfect.

A blade of light begins to cut through the darkness of the night. I am surprised to see that I am still sitting in front of my computer, believing instead that I traveled back in time to relive the tumultuous events that still shake everything around me. It's a good story, I think to myself. I wonder if I will ever write it down. For now, I must complete those darned recipes, before the sun rises and a new day begins.

3
A FAMILY AFFAIR

It has been seriously high tension at the magazine for the past week, and I am pleased to have an excuse to leave early. Unlike my sisters, the staff seems afraid to talk to me, the recent events as ugly as things get in gourmet cuisine publishing. Not that I'm looking forward to going to Nora's either. At least I have the 45-minute drive to clear my head.

I had recently published an article about one-upmanship among younger chefs, and how that was negatively impacting the level of art in our culinary community. It included a mention of one of the rising stars in our city. My point was the bigger issue of over-the-top cuisine, but it's true that I did not speak very kindly of him, and he really didn't like it.

The young chef publicly called me the has-been that never was, flaming me across more social media than I knew existed. It created quite the storm, not only at my magazine, but also throughout the restaurant world. He used his huge audience and willing media attention to express his rage at what he took as my defamation of his skills.

The magazine is still conflicted about responding or not, and so we all stew in this hot water, waiting for someone to do something. Most people think that someone is me.

The truth is that I know chefs; I used to be one. I know the industry rewards hot-headedness. This young man just felt his 15 minutes of fame being threatened by some nobody and lashed out. It really isn't as dramatic as everyone is making it out to be, but no one wants to be left out of the conversation, so a slew of media has been devoted to this ridiculous battle. He and I have become the polarizing points for anyone who has an opinion about food. There are those who see his behavior as histrionic, and are extremely insulted on my behalf. Then there are those who took my commentary personally, as if I had called their children dumb and ugly. I've been doing what I do best – staying silent.

I only hope my sisters haven't caught wind of this scandal. It will be yet another point on which to berate me.

I arrive at Nora's house, the implicit shared ground for all family matters, to find my two sisters sitting in the living room looking very serious. The only one missing is Sam, Nora's longtime partner. Something big is about to go down – I can feel it in the room. Lizzy, my expressive baby sister, is trying to hold the solemnity, but I know she will be the first to crack.

The questions begin almost immediately. Why aren't I showing any emotion or taking action to resolve all the messes in my life? How am I tolerating all these personal attacks? Why aren't I defending myself? How can I let him call me a no-talent nobody?

I find it all too ridiculous and childish to respond to.

"What happened to you?" Lizzy asks through the tears that start falling almost immediately. "You used to be the most passionate person I'd ever met. You loved food like most people love sex."

"Maybe just how you love sex, Lizzy," I remind my historically horny sister.

"Whatever. Now you don't even care that your entire reputation as a chef was just defamed and the work you're doing now is being totally ridiculed. Did you die in that divorce? What happened, Nik? What happened?"

I don't understand. I made a series of decisions, quite good I thought, to save my family. To move into a life that's much more reasonable and realistic. What is Lizzy saying? That my passion has died?

"I love what I do," I say in a soft voice, not quite sure how much I believe it. "It's just this guy is a wack-job, probably on his way to rehab as we speak. Why should I get all riled up about what he's saying?" I am genuinely curious.

"Because it's true," Nora says in an even softer voice. This makes Lizzy start crying harder.

I look around in confusion. Is this really happening? Am I being punked? How can they think the awful things that man had said were true? My feelings are hurt more by that quiet statement then by all the all-cap tweets put out by the angry chef.

Nora begins again. "We love you so much, Nik. You were the one who lived her dream. Defied convention and did something you were really, really good at, not just what you were expected to." My older sister speaks from experience, I admit.

"Ever since the divorce, and your working at that magazine, it's as if you put your soul in cold storage. You just work and take care of the girls and have no life. Do you even do anything you love anymore?"

"I LOVE MY GIRLS!!!!" It's much louder than I intend. Everyone is shocked. "Why are you doing this to me? Isn't it bad enough that I had to be publicly humiliated? Now my family has to tell me what a loser I am too? Are you guys for real???"

"We just want the old Monique back," Lizzy says. "My big sister who was my hero and my inspiration and everything I wanted to be when I grew up. Now you're gone. You're nearly invisible."

I begin to cry.

"Even the girls notice, you know," Nora says. "They say you're not as much fun. Claire says it's because you have a serious job now and you have to be a serious person. But that's not who you are. You are a wild, crazy, creative woman. Who was born free and unique, like a fairy or a mermaid."

That's the last straw. "How dare you!!!! To bring up my kids??? You have no fucking idea what I've been through and what I had to do just to survive. My family is doing GREAT now. Better than we ever have. We are happy and stable and we get to see each other and I'm not working crazy hours...

Why am I even explaining myself to you? You spent your whole lives just doing what you were told, not a fucking creative or free bone in your entire bodies, and you sit there and insult me? You wouldn't last a day in my shoes. Not even 5 minutes. So maybe you should start looking at your own pathetic piss-ass excuses for lives before you start insulting mine."

I rise off the couch. "I don't need to listen to this. I will never forgive you. Never."

Lizzy is sobbing so hard I think she might gag or throw up. Nora looks at me pleadingly. What does she want from me? To admit they are right? Never.

Lizzy begins pleading. "No, Nik. No. You can't leave. You're the best mother I know. The best one I've ever known and the best sister too. You can't leave and you can't hate us. I need you Nik! I need you now. I can't do it without you."

"Not now, Lizzy," Nora says with a slow deep voice.

"What the fuck are you two talking about???" I ask, frozen in my path towards the door.

"I'M PREGNANT, Nik. Really pregnant. I can't do it without you."

"No fucking way," I say, while finding somewhere to set myself down again.

We sit silently. Well nearly silently, as Lizzy is still sobbing and Nora is whispering to her, "It's ok sweet girl, it's ok. We're going to be there for you, ok? You're not alone. You're not alone."

I can't believe it. My baby sister, pregnant. No boyfriend that I've heard of. Holy shit. And her crazy career in advertising. What the hell is she going to do?

"How far along?" is all I can ask.

"Almost 10 weeks."

"Holy shit." She doesn't show at all. But maybe that explains why she's been looking so busty lately.

"That's not why we're here," says Nora, the pain-in-the-ass voice of reason. Always so fucking rational. I hate that about her.

"So why **are** we here?" I can't help the bitterness in my voice.

Nora clears her voice. "We're here because our sister needs help. And that's you we're talking about Monique. We can see the girl we have all known and loved just dying in there. You look nearly the same on the outside, but we know you're not the same on the inside. Why won't you let us in? It's ok if you have to live a lie, Nik, but you don't have to live it with us."

Nobody speaks for so long that my words startle everyone. "I'm not dying, I'm living. And I like my job, I really do. The girls and I are doing great. We are happy and healthy and living our lives. You have no right to say otherwise.

Maybe when they're a bit older, I can go back to the kitchen. For now, it's just not appropriate. I don't see how you can't understand that! Who wants a mother that comes home at 2am every night? It's completely ridiculous to even contemplate. There's a season for everything and right now it's about my family. There will be a season for me. Again."

"When?" Lizzy manages to say between her subdued sobs.

"I can't answer that! When it feels right."

"Who's the father Lizzy?" I need to move attention off of me.

"It's Mike. You don't know him. It was quick, and he pretty much told me he didn't want anything to do with me."

"She hasn't told him," adds Nora.

"What??? You have to tell him!"

"Why? So he can reject me even worse? No thanks. I can do it on my own. At least I think I can. I don't know..."

We all exhale together.

"I wish Danny was here," she says. Our brother. Our beloved baby brother, who died right before Mom and Dad. No brother has ever been so loved, and so wonderful. I think about him every day, and miss him even more often.

He had been our mediator for most of our lives. The voice of practicality and magic, all at the same time. He had a way of saying the most ridiculous things in a way that made you absolutely believe him. During the numerous girl wars that erupted in our house, he would take us all out in the woods and pretend to do an incantation to cure us all of the devil energy he claimed had taken us over. We would invariably end up in a huge giggle pile on the forest floor and spend the night picking leaves and twigs out of our hair.

The emptiness since he died has not shrunk a single inch. He was our boy, in a house so full of women.

He seemed to always have the answers to anything. He would know what to tell Lizzy about the baby, and he would know how to soothe my hurt feelings.

Danny understood me. My sweet baby brother, who felt about the ocean the way I felt about the kitchen, was the first to really *get* me. He explained to the others what I could not verbalize, until I had gotten successful enough that he didn't have to.

I wonder what he would think of my life now, since I've let go of *the dream*. He would have to understand that I made this choice for my family. That it was the right and reasonable thing to do.

Nora breaks me out of my reverie. "You know what Danny would say? He would say, 'You need to just get the devil out of you. Go outside and sing until your throats are all sore. Then come in, each do at least one shot of whisky and then lay in bed together.'"

Norah knew him the longest and it showed. She could channel him as needed. That's exactly what he would have said.

"You're right," I say.

They both look at me, as if I've just snapped out of a trance. They wait on my next words, but I have none.

"Ok, then... whiskey anyone? Except you Lizzy. Sorry," offers Nora.

"Fuck you," she says.

"No whiskey needed," I add. "But I do want to understand why you called me here tonight. Do you really think my life is so fucked up? Are my daughters damaged from all the hell we went through?"

"No, no, no..." Lizzy begins to cry again. "We LOVE you Nik. So much. We just wanted you to hear that YOU'RE not alone. You think you have to do everything on your own, and you don't. We're here and you never ask for help. We can help with the girls, or money or whatever you need. We just want you to be happy again."

"What makes you think I'm not happy?"

"Because you're not. It's as simple as... like when you tried being a blonde for a little while. It didn't look bad, but we knew it wasn't actually who you are," Nora says.

"And you need to get laid more," says Lizzy.

"Look where that got you, missy." We all laugh at that one. Nora's stiffness softens and Lizzy's tear-stained face can't hold back a chuckle. It feels like we've torn down the walls and opened the doors.

"Are the girls with Jeff tonight?" asks Nora.

"Yup."

"Great. You are going to stay here tonight. We all are. Just like we used to do, all curled up in Mom and Dad's giant bed. Except it's my giant bed, but whatever. We have to stick together. We're it ladies, the last of the Malones. And Lizzy is going to be a mom, and Nik is going to go back to cooking, and we all need lots of help and we're all we have. It's time to go."

With that, Nora walks toward the bedroom. Like good little soldiers, we follow.

"I'll get the water," I say, and fill 3 huge glasses with water for our bedtime thirst. We had all inherited this love of water from our mom, needing to drink constantly, day and night.

We laugh and cry and sleep very little. We craft the speech Lizzy will give to her boss about being pregnant, compose the letter to the father, and hatch a plan for my illustrious return back to the kitchen. I'll start small, maybe just a part-time gig to get my skills back, and slowly make my way up the ladder again. My girls will spend more time with their beloved aunties.

Being a chef is a lot like being a celebrity - you're only as good as your last movie or meal - and I haven't cooked in a long time. Other than the recent hooplah, I am dead to the cooking world. I will have to prove my chops once again.

I am so tickled with excitement that even after my sisters have fallen asleep, I stay awake. So many different ideas flow through my mind. I can find a place that just does breakfast and lunch. A small place with exemplary food without all the pressure. Or I can become a private chef, even though that's less interesting. My ultimate dream is to run the kitchen at a B&B, maybe even in wine country, a few hours away from our home in San Francisco.

Jeff and I had spent many hours plotting out our retirement in Sonoma - he would be the concierge doctor in a quaint little town, running our world-famous B&B, and I would turn out the most fabulous food the world had ever seen, in very small scale.

That dream always brought a smile to my face, no matter how distant it seemed. I could almost taste it.

But there are so many problems. First, I have no money to start a B&B and now that Jeff is starting a family with his nurse-girlfriend, he will have no interest in funding my little venture. And I am fairly certain that he no longer has any interest in moving. Since we share custody of the girls, neither of us can go very far without the other's consent. How can this ever work?

Despite the impossibility of it all, I eventually fall asleep. We wake up in age order with Nora up to make the coffee, and Lizzy likely sleeping till noon. I have a copy deadline today, but have already completed the piece and can have a leisurely morning. It's nice to be with my sisters again. It's been such a long time since we've had agenda-less time together.

A pang from last night hits me. I never responded to what they were saying to me, just picked up and went along with the plan. Was it real? Do they really want to help me get back into cooking? It seems like such a long shot, especially with their already full lives.

As Lizzy rolls out of bed, we can hear her stumble into the bathroom and throw up. Nora is disgusted. I am excited. I am going to be an auntie! After my oldest sister declared she was living child-free, I gave up hope. But now... there is a chance.

"Should we go help her?" I ask.

"That's revolting. She'll come out when she's ready."

"Aaaaahhh... the voice of compassion."

Lizzy comes out and Nora hands her a tea that I hadn't even seen her make.

"Thanks. Sorry about that," knowing Nora's aversion to bodily functions. "It was worse for me, in case you were wondering."

I give her a hug. "You know that means the baby is good and strong, right? It's what you want. And it will pass, maybe even in the next week or so. My morning sickness went away right on my 12th week, each time. It was a miracle!"

"Let's hope..."

"Shall we go out for breakfast?" Nora asks.

"Just toast for me, thanks," says Lizzy, still slightly green.

"Why don't I make something?" They both stare at me, open-jawed, not trying to hide their disbelief.

"Fuck you both," is all I can say. "If you don't watch out, I just might poison your betraying evil asses, assuming that Nora actually has any food in her house."

"Feast your eyes on this, Sis." A flourishing sweep of the refrigerator door reveals a bounty of goodies.

Lizzy and I are both incredulous. "Where did all that come from?" I ask.

"Sam hired someone to fill my fridge. It's nice. I like it."

My oldest sister has one of the oddest lives I have ever known. She followed in the footsteps of our father and became a scientist. A very successful one.

She had gotten tenure in one of the most prestigious universities in the country and is working her way up the ladder there too. Nothing short of a Nobel will stop my sister.

Her partner, whom she has sworn she will never marry, is in the philosophy department, the complete counterpoint to her obsessive logic. We all love Sam, sometimes more than we love Nora. We can't believe that she found this amazing man, who loves her more than life itself, and agrees to all her crazy demands.

They would keep separate houses, she demanded. And vacation separately at least once a year. No kids. That was an absolute. He is mesmerized by her, much like our father was mesmerized by our mother. He finds her infinitely charming, intelligent and beautiful.

And now he is making sure she's fed. Unlike Lizzy or me, Nora has a tendency to get too skinny. She forgets to eat (imagine that!!), sometimes for days at a time, hunkered down in the lab, afire with the newest trail to track down the common genetic links between widely varied species.

Like the rest of us, she also holds this soft, secret sadness, but hers is harder to diagnose. On the surface, she's created the life of her dreams, including the perfect man and career. She's in excellent health, meal skipping aside, and doesn't want for anything financially. The sadness is nearly imperceptible, and reminds me of our mother.

"You did mean breakfast today, right?" says a sarcastic Nora.

I realize I've been standing in front of the open refrigerator for minutes.

"Extra poison in yours, bitch," I say with a wink.

And then I begin. Cooking to me feels like music to the rest of the family. I don't have their musical skill (although I try) but I can make a symphony on a plate or palate.

Nora's kitchen is stocked with the best of everything, as expected, and I'm excited to create. Fancy food is not my thing, but I am thrilled by absolutely delicious, simple food that makes you feel like someone loves you, not just that someone is trying to impress you.

I make eggs, French toast, fruit salad and smoothies as well as stir-fried greens, curry rice and ginger soup. I figure that Nora and Sam can enjoy any of the leftovers.

Even Lizzy eats, in small tentative bites. I am filled with love for my sisters.

That feeling of feeding my family, of coming together to share what nourishes us, of rediscovering our humanity and our neediness and our hunger, is like a deep breath. I wonder when I will be fully ready to respond to my sisters' plea to really live my authentic life. It will likely be some time.

For now I have a plan to create.

First I have to call Emile, my friend and mentor, who also happens to be the most well-connected person in the culinary world. He'll know where to start. Maybe even be happy that I want to go back. He's always been my biggest fan, if not my best lover.

I start to feel a tickle of excitement and a tremor of trepidation. What's next for me?

The reality of the day arrives suddenly. Phones start ringing, schedules become important and obligations come to call. The end of breakfast and the beginning of the rest of the day come so swiftly that it's almost as if the morning never happened. Now it's time to get on with our full lives.

On my drive back to the city, I feel the urge to deal with the situation around my inflammatory article and the angry chef. Should I wait until I've re-established myself as a chef? Or would that take too long? The world (or the small part of the world that cares about such things) is waiting to hear from me and I've been mostly unwilling to engage. But perhaps it's time to be heard.

I arrive home a few hours before the girls, but spend most of the time staring at my computer screen. What to say to someone who has thrown down the gauntlet that you were not ready to pick up? What to say to defend your honor against petulance, immaturity and unreasonable competition? I'm not interested in going after this guy. I know he just feels attacked and is defending himself, no matter how excessive the response.

I simply want to state my case, unapologetically, and let the matter die its inevitable death. But where to start? Slowly the words come to me, about the integrity of food and the subjectivity of taste and the power of free speech. Then I begin to feel how much I love food and cooking and the business of eating and the words begin to pour from me.

I've been obsessed with food most of my life. In a good way. I love everything about it - the alchemy of bringing simple ingredients together to create something much greater than its parts, the understanding of how food forms culture and determines health. My sister Nora used to say that I would have made a great chemist, considering how similar the two activities are, but I have no interest in science. I want to make something that is beautiful and delicious. Her discoveries as a biologist may be changing the world, but I want to feed people. To nourish them.

I can feel it in my body when I think about my old life, as a chef. And not just any chef, but one whose rise to fame had been charmed. My family of artists and scientists hardly understood me, the one whose favorite room in the house was the kitchen, where magic was made. But it made perfect sense to me, because art, science and magic all lived in that room, where the simplest materials could become something that made people happy.

My sisters are wrong. My work as a writer is not merely obligation and the need to make a living. I really do find joy and value in it, and stand by my choice. At the time, trying to survive the implosion of my family, being a chef felt impractical. Certainly not what a single mom should be doing to support her family. I was going to survive the awful divorce, and create stability for myself and my family. Soft dreams gave way to hard realities and I found a way to make it work. I walked away from the stove and into the office.

The position at the magazine was a miracle find, after all. But it isn't my heart's desire. That I have to agree. Do I feel it is sucking my soul dry? No, not at all. But am I just fooling myself? Have I moved so far from my authentic expression that I can't even tell anymore?

The shrill ring of my alarm surprises me. It's time for school pick-ups. I'm looking forward to giving my girls a loving squeeze. They are the light of my life, and even if I never do anything of value in my life I know I achieved something by bringing these remarkable people into the world.

The rest of the day unfolds into ordinariness. There are activities, dinner, homework and then baths and bedtime.

I spend extra time snuggling my girls and we say our grate-fulls. I let them know, as I do every night, that I am deeply grateful for them in my life. They talk about not having too much homework, doing well on surprise quizzes, and having parents who love them. I can't hold it in and tell them about my plan to go back to cooking. Claire had known me back in those early days, but Lola does not really understand. We both explain to her that Mama used to be a famous cook (ok, we embellish a bit). She seems to find it unbelievable.

Claire begins to describe how she saw me, before the big change.

"Mama was really popular. She worked in big and famous restaurants too, and sometimes famous people would come and eat there. She was a really good chef."

I can't help but smile at my little girl, who never once mentioned my previous profession or indicated that she thought I did anything of interest or importance. Maybe this change won't be so hard after all.

4

RULE OF THREES

I barely recover from 'The Intervention' and the ego battle at the magazine before the next storm hits. Or storm cluster, to be more precise.

When I see the middle school's number flashing on my phone, I'm sure it's not good. And I'm right.

My talented Claire has always had a song on her lips, and often forgets that she is singing or humming. The whole family, and all her friends, understand, and love this quirky quality. Apparently one of the boys at school didn't find it quite as charming, and smacked her across the face – hard. By the time I get to her school, the pink marks have faded, covered now with the tracks of her tears. The school official is devastated about the alleged violence, but considering he can't get a straight story out of the hysterical participants and bystanders, decides to make it a no-fault issue.

I'm furious, but thankfully think better than exacting my own revenge on that little boy.

"Are you ok, sweetie?" I ask as she sits quietly in the car.

"Yeah, Mama. I'm fine. It doesn't really sting anymore."

"Do you think your singing was bothering him for some reason?" I'm not sure where I'm going with these questions, but my curiosity is killing me. "What exactly happened?"

"I don't know, Mama. He just got so mad when he asked me to be quiet, and I wouldn't. I didn't even realize I was humming, but I guess he could hear it."

"That must have been awful baby. I wish I could take it all away for you." I do.

"I think he just forgot I was a girl. I mean, that's how all the boys act toward each other. They're always hitting and wrestling, like bears or something. I think he just forgot for a second... that I wasn't a bear."

My wise girl.

"I really appreciate how you're being so cool, and fair about all this. I'm very proud of you."

"I know, Mama."

We decide to pick up Lola and got some ice cream. It's definitely a good day for ice cream.

The visual of boys as bears is going to stay with me for some time. It reinforces everything I feel about men and betrayal: Expressing the song in your heart gets you a smack across the face.

It's less than a week later when I see Jeff's number on my phone in the middle of the day. It's unlike him to call during his workday. I assume he butt-dialed me.

"Hi there. What's up?" I ask, expecting silence on the other end.

"Hi Nik."

Something's wrong. His voice is off.

"It's my dad, Nik. He's gone." The breath leaves my body in a whoosh, punctuated by Jeff's sobs. His father is one of my favorite people on the planet. He had been there for me even through the worst of our divorce.

"No… that can't be right. No, Jeff."

"It's true, Nik. Mom said he was feeling tired, and laid down for a nap, which he would never do. Then his heart stopped. Everyone thinks it was painless. I don't know…"

"Oh my God, Jeff. I can't believe it. Can I do anything for you? Do you need me to take care of anything?" How quickly we fall into our old connection.

"Patti's getting our stuff together now." Funny, I had forgotten all about her. "We're flying out in a few hours. I just thought you'd want to know."

"Of course. Thanks for calling. Do you want me to tell the girls, or do you want to?"

"Why don't you do it Nik? I just don't think I could keep it together for them."

"Anything you need, Jeff. Will you let me know when the service is? Maybe we can come out."

"It's so far, Nik." They live across the country. "You don't have to. But I'll let you know."

"Ok. Safe flight, ok?"

"Thanks. Talk soon."

The feeling of the chair around me makes me realize that I have sat down. My body has lost the ability to hold itself up, and the tears begin to flow. The stream of grief begins with Jeff's father, but moves quickly to my own parents, and to Danny. So many people gone, it's too much to process.

My heart breaks for Jeff. I know exactly what it's like to lose a parent unexpectedly. But he's always been stronger than me.

I can remember so clearly the first time I saw Jeff. It was my first week cooking at a prestigious restaurant, and getting *paid*, after having apprenticed for the hottest chef in the city. Of the four apprentices they selected from my cooking school, they chose me to continue on. It was nothing short of a miracle.

Jeff's arm was wrapped securely around a woman whose proportions made me wonder how she didn't topple over. I had this natural mistrust of 'breast men', easily explained by my own lacking in that department - it was all legs and bottom for me – but he caught and kept my attention anyway.

I couldn't decide if he was handsome, or just so blatantly confident that I couldn't help myself from staring as he walked towards me. They sat in front of the open kitchen, in the most prized seats in the restaurant, only given to very special customers, so I knew he was either important or rich. Probably both.

He oozed cool flawlessness. I was a nervous wreck, convinced that any wrong move, no matter how slight, would get me kicked out on my butt. I have never experienced anywhere more competitive than a fine dining kitchen, and all eyes were on the new girl.

His eyes were certainly on me as well, to the dismay of his pouting date. He asked about all the dishes I was working on, and then wanted to know about how I started cooking. Speaking was limited, as everything was so busy, but he stayed attentive.

As soon as his date headed towards the bathroom, he slipped me his card, making some excuse about the possibility of my needing a good surgeon should one of those knives slip. I wasn't sure how an orthopedic surgeon would re-attach one of my severed digits, but thankfully it never came to that.

Of course, so consumed with my new job, working 12-15 hour days, I never called him. And there was the complication that he had been with a woman when we met. Then he started coming to the restaurant regularly, by himself, and sitting at the counter. The fourth time I saw him, he asked me out.

As soon as he arrived at my apartment to pick me up that night, I knew I would have to up my game. This guy was super smooth, and I was an awkward mess. The only love in my life to that point had been my career, and I had never met anyone who understood what it meant to be passionately in love with your job.

He felt the same way about medicine as I did about food, and could talk about surgery like a child talking about candy. It was his life's dream to be a doctor, and I could only guess how talented he was. He treated me like a grown-up. Not like a new chef, or an inexperienced girl, but like a grown woman whose opinions mattered and whose dreams were as important as his own.

Our courtship was slowed down by our busy schedules, but the commitment was clear, nearly from the beginning. Despite the romance of the early days, Jeff never actually proposed. We just sat down one day and started planning our wedding. As obvious and expected as our summer vacation in France.

Our lives settled into an ease, lubricated by frequent separations and our own passionate immersions into our careers. When we were actually together, it was nice enough. Jeff was interested in and supportive of my life, our families got along quite well, and we never lacked for anything. Perhaps I didn't notice how little intimacy there was, as I was so absorbed and fulfilled by my work. My dream was expanding, and the world was accommodating. I was being touted as one of the next generation of great chefs. There was talk about creating a signature restaurant. Just for me.

Things began to change between us after Claire was born. I never realized how much I could love another human being until my daughter came into my life. It made the feelings for my husband even more painful in comparison.

Being her mother should have been the easiest job in the world. Claire was a gift of a child, so easy-going, and beautiful. I knew immediately that naming her after my mother had been the right thing to do. She had this other-worldliness about her, like my brother Danny had, too.

Her skill with music, however, came directly from her grandmother. Claire's constant stream of songs provided the soundtrack for our strange, disconnected family.

I was equally mesmerized and terrified by this tiny creature who was now mine to protect, torn between wanting to be with her every moment, and wanting to be living my dream life as a chef. Neither part of my life felt right anymore – my time at the restaurant was tainted with an urgency to be with my baby, and my time with Claire would leave me with rising anxiety about my ability to be a mother, my leaving behind the only thing in my life I had ever been really good at, and the impossibility of how I could possibly do everything that was being asked of me. The internal battle would rage every time I had to leave her, but every night (or morning as it happened on occasion) I would come home to my baby and know that it was all as it was supposed to be. At least for a few hours.

In a strange role reversal, Claire became my source of solace and comfort. She had this intuitive sense that told her exactly what to do and say. Sometimes I would feel embarrassed to be the weak and needy one, but had to accept that that's how it was for us.

I wanted it all to work, although the unlikelihood was staring me right in the face. The crazy hours Jeff and I were tied to were not conducive to the round-the-clock care a baby needed, and tensions built quickly about our respective responsibilities. Jeff was taking on more and more at the hospital, and even traveling to train other doctors and speak at conferences. He was proud of how well he was providing for our family, even if not in person. Although my culinary star kept getting brighter, it didn't mean any fewer hours for me either.

"It's time for you to leave your frivolous career behind and stay home to take care of our child, Monique," he eventually said.

That's when I stopped speaking, so overtaken by betrayal. Jeff grew more and more insistent, my suffering apparently not a consideration. How could I leave the only thing in my life, other than my daughter, that filled my heart with joy? Yes, it was an enormous amount of work, and yes it brought in nearly no money and was very stressful and time-consuming. But it was my life. It was how I defined myself - I was a chef, before anything else. How dare he demand I leave my career?

He grew louder and I grew silent. He grew larger, and I shrank into my two unsatisfying worlds of mother and chef.

Silence became my husband's lover. A lifetime of meticulously chosen words, and a short period of incoherent raging, left me mute. No need to wonder what happens after one screams so violently that the voice fails. Silence, of course.

Whose hand is over my mouth, I wondered, powerless to move my jaw. Being incapable of complaining also meant no oral sex. He would suffer for what he had done.

By not speaking, I could bear the dishonesty. By feigning agreement, I would keep the peace. By locking my jaw, I could stop being force fed his chilling torment.

Silence cooked for him, silence slept with him and silence hung on his arm, right alongside the Rolex, neither making even a tick.

Maybe I had used up my quota of words. A bit soon, I thought, but not impossible. Or maybe, by using words like weapons, which I had done with so many others, I had broken some covenant and been banned to the land of the speechless.

Be seen and not heard, resurrected from childhood. Silent AND deadly.

How much venom could be produced with a wordless gaze, a tight-lipped grimace, a rigid backed response? A nearly fatal dose, I came to understand, without the need to bare the fangs locked behind the prison of my mouth.

Everyone could see the cause of this strange symptom, the locking of my jaw. But I dared not even think the thought – my life was sealing my lips shut.

What would I have to admit, about my own part in the tragic farce, to say – "He did this, and I let him?"

Silence was the price for security, the counterfeit for connection, as valuable as any of the constant lies. Whether spoken or not, dishonesty was our secret code.

I would win this one. If shutting up and shutting off were the rules of engagement, I would be the silent victor.

"You won't talk to me," he would say. *No shit*, I thought, and that was that. I won the round, again.

But he changed the rules, so quickly I could not veer from the strategy – to manipulate him into acquiescence. I rounded the bend to find that he had left me, emotionally.

Unable to bear the hypocrisy, or the silence of lies, he stopped playing mid-game, took his heart and left. The only pleas were silent as I realized it was my own hand over my mouth.

When lies are all you tell, what is the value of your word? When the truth is too hard to bear what is the value of your life?

Does silence burn in the consumption of rage or stand at the doorway to ecstasy? Who holds the barometer, the perfectly precise gauge of 'rightness' by which to assess the opening and closing of one's mouth… the opening and closing of one's heart?

Fill the hole with whatever is around to keep it busy, or seal it so tightly for no trespassing, I told myself. Breathe, moan, whisper, cry, scream, laugh. But speak not or forever hold your peace.

In a rare moment of courage, when the rift had grown enormous, I began to plot my escape from the marriage. Jeff had already commenced his next relationship, with no concern whether I knew or not. Not sure how I would manage financially or as a single mom, but I could not take the hostile environment in my own house and the slow crushing of my dream.

The whole process with the lawyer was much easier than I thought. As I was about to secretly file papers, Jeff and I had an unexpected reconnection, courtesy of a wine-tasting at my favorite vineyard and an especially soft energy from my husband. Our sex life had dwindled to almost nothing since Claire was born, partly because of the changes in my body and the exhaustion, but mostly because of our toxic relationship. I considered myself nearly asexual during those years. No desire, no thoughts, no interest.

Our lovemaking was beautiful that night, reminiscent of the early days of our courtship. We were in no rush, as Claire was at a friend's house, and neither of us had to work in the morning.

We took our time, and rediscovered each other. Things between us got a bit better after that. I noticed that he was more helpful around the house, less denigrating about my work, and even kinder to our daughter. My fantasies turned to the rebirth of our marriage, the return of the life I thought I wanted.

It all shifted again when I realized I was pregnant. No way could I handle another kid, now that Claire was in preschool. I was looking forward to greater independence and more time for myself, if even just to sleep. No possibility for that to happen with another baby on the way.

I panicked and withdrew again. Jeff reverted to his previous coldness and disdain. We fell into our old patterns like a hole in the road. I waited a very long time to tell him I was pregnant, even to the point that strangers began to notice. I was too far along to do anything about it. I just kept willing it to go away and at the same time, knowing somehow that this baby would save me. It would prevent me from continuing down this path of a loveless marriage and self-hatred.

When I told him I was pregnant, he barely changed expression, as if I had just announced we were having lasagna for dinner. He nodded and said, "Great. Maybe we'll have a boy this time," then went back to what he was reading.

I thought the crack in my heart would be irreparable. I didn't mind anger or other strong emotions, but apathy was my kryptonite. I felt my face burn and my heart shatter. Part of me wanted him to be furious. To rail and cry about the absurdity of bringing another human being into this farce of a marriage. Part of me wanted my transformation into a mother again to create a shift for him, back to the man who wanted me so deeply, and cared.

There was no way I could be in this marriage one minute longer. But there was no leaving now. What would I do? Move into a shelter? I could not support myself with my work, at least not the way we had been living, and I could not put in any more hours with a small child to take care of. I didn't want to assume that Jeff would take care of us, financially, given his feelings about the situation. I had heard too many horror stories about divorces going terribly wrong.

Lola was born in the middle of the night, after everyone was already exhausted from a challenging day of labor. She came out of me like a lion, full of roar and fury, the scream impossible not to hear.

It was much harder than with Claire, and made worse by the fact that everyone had said that the second would be so much easier. I resented Jeff's presence during the birth, but he seemed insistent on staying. My body was trying to birth a baby and my heart was trying to flee - from the man I no longer loved or wanted to be with. From the prospect that I would have to leave my world of cooking. And from yet another life in my hands, when I was making such a mess of the one I already had.

Holding Lola in my arms, I found a source of strength that transcended my exhausted body and beleaguered mind. That night, after cradling my new baby girl, my second daughter, the mother bear arose. I knew I would not raise my girls in a house of mediocrity, lovelessness or powerlessness.

"I'm not doing this anymore. I'm leaving. With the girls."

Jeff held his newborn daughter and cried, knowing the inevitable had just happened. We spent the next several days in a peaceful silence, enjoying the short time as a family that would soon dissolve. I appreciated the quiet and the lack of conflict or interrogation. Little did I know that Jeff was plotting a full-scale attack. He would do anything to prevent me from leaving, either kindly or not.

He offered me anything I wanted. Separate rooms, money, time at a prestigious cooking school in Europe. All I wanted to do was leave, but he would not have it. The break-up of his family was not on the very specific agenda for his life.

The divorce raged on for 3 years, while Jeff tried to find any means to pull me back in. He knew better than to play the child card - he loved his daughters and knew that he could never take them away from their mother. For this, I am eternally grateful, even though I didn't know it at the time. This would become the thread that eventually rebuilt our relationship as co-parents and friends.

My emotional departure was mirrored by his physical one, as he moved on to his next relationship. That act, painful as it was for me, was the first sign that the divorce would actually happen, which had been unclear before then.

When I was finally free, I had to completely undo and redo my life, alone with the girls. Restaurant hours would no longer work with my abbreviated family and I had very little money to hire a round-the-clock nanny. My dearest friend Emile, the man who knew everyone in the culinary world, found me a job at a national food magazine, as a writer. He knew I had been writing informally for some time, and enjoyed it.

The move to journalism would solve all the problems - a steady paycheck, stability and best of all, hours that work with raising two young children. Without even thinking about it, I said yes. Exuberantly. It was the answer to my dreams.

I went off to my new corporate job happily. It was the solution I had been searching for, without knowing it existed. It kept me in that world I so cherished, utilized my writing skills, put food on the table and me at home with my kids. I could not believe my luck.

The divorce became final, by default, as it happened in our state, on an anticlimactic day. I told my sisters, and poured myself a beer. It had been an extremely long and bitter road. I had lost nearly everything - my kindness, compassion, perseverance and self-awareness - but I still had my beautiful girls. And the strength to wake up another day and do it again. In the scheme of things, it could have been worse. Not much, but some.

Now, here we are. Making our way back to a place of respect, and even love. Without him, I never would have these human beings in my life – my beloved girls. My heart aches for the loss of his father. And mine.

The girls and I hunker down in our own processes of hurting and healing. We talk about all the grandparents they have lost, and how it makes them feel. I don't even pretend to be the strong one, my own grief relentlessly rising to the surface like a thousand tiny bubbles.

5

VEGAS, BABY

Even with Emile's help, it's a tough road back to the kitchen. I swallow my pride a hundred times, as chefs I can out-cook with both hands behind my back decide I am not good enough. Or too old. Or too constrained. I am worse than old news – I am no news at all.

I get my first 'yes' in the most unlikely place, at a hot new restaurant that had just lost two kitchen staff that week. Their desperation is my salvation, and the chef agrees to take me on as an apprentice. There is no money, of course, but the experience will get me back in top shape in lightning speed.

I work at the magazine during the day and spend a few evenings every week at the restaurant. None of the kids working beside me have ever heard of me, but my skills come back quickly. I resist saying, "Do you know who I am??!" about a thousand times during my comeback.

In the moments when I tie my apron, and unroll my knife bag, I feel alive again. All the chaos – prep chefs busily working in the back, produce delivery people in and out, even the business guys yelling about the books in the office – fade into a distant hum as I find my own rhythm. All I hear is the sound of my knives against the sharpening steel, the whoosh of the gas ovens catching, and the sizzle of my creations. I begin to know joy again, in a way that I had forgotten for so long.

A new me is emerging. I can't help but sense that there are more surprises to come.

No one, however, is particularly surprised when Nora gets nominated for a national science award, but the fact that she offers to take us all to Las Vegas for the ceremony makes us jump up and down like game show contestants. Lizzy is finally moving past her morning sickness and wants to go, maybe as her last hurrah before she gets too big. We promise to fund as much spa time as she needs. Nora forbids Sam from coming and dubs this 'girls' weekend'. I'm sure he's disappointed but there's no changing Nora's mind once she decides something.

Nora had gotten us adjoining rooms at the hottest hotel, and planned the entire itinerary around enjoying the best restaurants and clubs. The schedule is packed, with very little time for actual sleeping. I know I will need multiple outfits per day.

I'm excited. Maybe more than I should be. I don't care that the chef at the restaurant is annoyed about my needing time off. I don't care that Jeff is questioning why I need to go to Las Vegas. I don't care that I don't have anything cool to wear.

I haven't been out in a big way for far too long. I spend so much time going through my closet trying to find something acceptable (in Vegas terms) for the long weekend that Claire declares we have to go shopping. I want to be a little bit racy, but not ridiculous, for a woman of my age.

As I scrutinize myself in the dressing room mirrors, I acknowledge that I'm doing OK. I've let my hair grow a bit longer, so that it's easier to tie back for the kitchen, and my face doesn't look quite as drawn as it has recently. There's a rosiness underneath my olive skin that looks good, I admit. My body has settled into a 40-something combination of strength and curves, which fills my clothes in an attractive way. Even if everything else was a wreck, I realize I still have those legs. The ones that make buying pants off the rack nearly impossible, but I have no doubt they are my strong suit.

Claire notices me looking pleased with myself.

"You are really beautiful, Mama. I like when you're this happy. And this is definitely a step up from your yoga pants and sweatshirts."

"You're right, sweetie. Thank you for helping me." I never think anyone notices my wardrobe, but my daughter apparently does. I sigh at the thought that maybe I should put a little more effort into my appearance.

"You should get dressed up more often. All these fancy clothes look so good on you!"

"Well, maybe one day I'll have a fancy life to warrant all these fancy clothes."

"I bet you will Mama. I bet you will. Now try on the stack over there. We've got lots more to do."

The shopping trip is fruitful - I put together several great outfits, even buy a celebratory pair of shoes. It isn't clear how I will actually walk around in them, but for those few moments that I am able to stay upright, I'm going to look fabulous!

I have to fly out on my own, the day after my sisters, as Jeff is travelling beforehand and I have to wait for him to return to watch the girls. My sisters call as they are settling into their rooms, and they can barely contain their glee. I can't understand what they are saying on the phone, there is such a din of laughter and music and... is that a man's voice I hear?

"What is going on there, ladies??" I ask.

"We couldn't wait for you to start the party could we, slow poke? Just get your ass here and you'll see for yourself." Lizzy, even without alcohol, is buzzing.

The day finally comes, my luggage filled with little black dresses, sequined stilettos and cherry red lipstick. Yes, I am going to party, as well as make some high profile connections. Vegas had become a culinary Mecca up there with New York and Paris, and with Emile's interventions, I am set up for VIP treatment wherever I want to go. Nora is suitably impressed. There might not be sleep in our schedule, but at least we are going to eat very well.

I realize how long it's been since I last travelled as I move in slow-motion through the airport. Everything is new and interesting. Even the crowds, unhappy people, and rude workers don't rile me. I am wearing my 'I am going to Vegas' grin, nearly as big as my head.

I made sure I began on the right foot by getting decked out for the flight, and I'm pleased I did. I don't mind that it's only a few hours – it's an opportunity for me to show up as the fabulous babe I am going to unveil in the lighted city. This is the beginning of my grand coming-out party.

I stop at an airport shop to buy a bottle of water. I must have begun daydreaming on line and am awoken from my Vegas fantasies by a deep, slightly accented voice saying, "Excuse me, ma'am. Excuse me, are you ready?"

I look ahead at the huge gap in the line ahead and the clearly impatient sales girl at the register. The gentle beckoning certainly did not come from her. I turn around to see a man smiling at me.

"I'm so sorry," I say breathlessly. Wow, he's very good looking. Too good looking. The kind of man with whom I tend to act like a complete idiot.

"Gosh I must have been daydreaming..."

"NEXT!!" comes the insistent urge from the cashier. I pay for my water and magazine, then walk out, afraid to look back at the man. *Wow*, is all I can think.

I arrive back at the gate just as boarding begins (my generous sister kind enough to have upgraded me to first class). I have to say, this is growing more and more perfect, as I settle into my big comfy seat and accept a glass of champagne from the attendant.

I realize, a bit too late, that I haven't set myself up well for the flight. I need to get my magazine out of my bag, put away my phone and buckle my seat belt. But all my hands are full. I sit, awkwardly, trying to figure out what to put down and how to juggle everything.

"Would you like some help?" someone asks. Not just someone, but that same voice from the store. Can it be?

I turn around to see one seat behind me, on the other side of the aisle, the gorgeous man with the beautiful smile. How does he know what I am doing? Is my clumsiness transmitting seats away?

I decide to bypass my potential embarrassment, as this is an omen of great things, and I'm not going to let *Monique the Dork* rule the day. *Monique the Goddess/Diva/Sex Kitten* is coming out to play. And play with this man I will.

"Why yes, I would," I say in as coy a voice as I can muster. Did that really come out of my mouth??? Holy shit, I'm embarrassed for myself already. But no, must keep going. No retreat.

"What can I do for you?" he asks, right back in that fucking sexy voice of his, so deep and tinted with just a hint of an accent. Italian? Or Spanish? Holy crap this man could probably talk me into an orgasm. Right here on this plane.

"Well, would you mind pulling my tray out for me? I seem to have a shortage of hands." I look up just in time to see the flight attendants eyeing me quizzically. I flash right back - *Back off bitches. He's mine.*

"Absolutely," he volunteers. He rises from his seat and is by my side in one easy step. He removes my elbow from the armrest and pulls out the small extension of the middle tray, which I've already filled with my phone and headphones.

I can smell him as he leans in to me, and think, this man cannot be for real. I am getting more and more turned on. I wonder if the lady sitting next to me would switch seats.

"Anything else I can do for you?" he asks with the most enticing smile I have ever seen. The champagne must be going to my head...

"Well, yes, since you asked. A refill would be wonderful," as I hand him my nearly empty champagne glass.

With that, he takes my glass, walks to the galley and asks the shocked attendants for more champagne. They admonish him to return to his seat, as we are about to take off. He smiles at them and they fill the glass without any more commentary. He is a charmer and knows it. I wonder if this guy is ever denied what he wants. Part of me wants to be the one who rejects him, but who am I kidding. This man could invite me into the airplane bathroom and I would probably go.

"Champagne for the beautiful lady." He stands in front of me, handing me my newly filled glass. Did he really just call me a beautiful lady? I try not to look so obvious while searching to see who else he could have been referring to. *What an ass I am*, I can't help but think.

He laughs softly.

"Why thank you. I will definitely recommend you for a generous raise." And I wink. Seriously, I wink. I must be channeling some celebrity vixen - something is fueling my newfound brazenness. We haven't even taken off yet, and it is already the most fun plane ride I have ever taken.

He returns to his seat and I look down, pretending to flip through my magazine. OH MY GOD, I think. I know I am breathing hard and try to calm myself down. *Take it easy, babe. I'm sure this guy is used to women falling all over him. Play it cool!*

I pretend to skim my magazine through the remainder of takeoff. Every now and then I feel like he's looking at me, but I dare not turn back and check. Too obvious, too desperate, even though I am both of those things. *Just keep reading*, I tell myself.

I remember my headphones and decide to put some music on. Yes, that will be just distracting enough to keep me from obsessing.

His hand is on my arm. HIS HAND IS ON MY ARM!!! I turn hesitatingly, removing my headphones as if in slow motion.

"Hi," I say.

"Hi." Then nothing. He smiles at me.

"My name is Marco. I, um, I'm going to a friend's wedding in Vegas. Not that you asked." He laughs at himself and shakes his head slightly. Maybe he's nervous too. Wow. This is good stuff.

"My name is Monique, though nearly everyone calls me Nik. My sister was nominated for a science research award and I'm going to the ceremony. My younger sister too. The three of us are having a bit of a girl's weekend I guess." I laugh shyly, wondering if he has any idea what girls do with a weekend in Vegas.

"Staying anywhere good?" he asks.

"We're at the Wynn, where the conference is."

"Great!" he says a bit too quickly. "That's actually where the wedding is. Have you been there? It's a beautiful hotel."

"I haven't been, no. But I hear good things. Then again is there anything in Vegas that's not amazing?"

"Good point," he agrees. "I am sure you and your sisters will add beauty and grace to anything there."

"Or maybe there will be 3 very drunk women, completely unused to all that glitz, making fools of themselves." *Did I really just say that?? Ughhhh. Get yourself together, girl.*

"You are very funny, Monique. And I really can't imagine that happening. So, what are the husbands doing with themselves?"

Wow. He is digging for info. My gosh, this is too much fun.

"Missing us," I say with a playful grin. His face falls, slightly. "Just kidding. No husbands between us."

"Lucky Vegas," he says flashing that smile again. This is too much. I am having such a great time with this guy that I forget to notice that he is totally out of my league. No, I'm not going to let that stop me. I'm going to rise to the occasion.

As I turn to respond to him, the flight attendant steps directly in my view. "Have you decided on your meal?" Snippy. Very snippy.

I order and let her finish her survey before turning back to Marco.

"Do you live in San Francisco, Marco?" I try to sound as nonchalant as possible.

"Yes, I do. I have an office in Argentina as well so I spend some time there."

"That's a wonderful combination of places to be. What do you do?" Cool and calm, not looking like I care too much.

"I'm an architect. Mostly private homes but a few public buildings. In the US and South America."

"That's very impressive. I've always been fascinated by architecture. It's such a cool mixture of art and science, don't you think? Creative and functional at the same time. Built anything I would have seen?"

"Well, maybe. We could turn around in Vegas and go to South America so I could show you myself."

OK, that's some serious flirting. And I can keep up. I might be rusty, but I'm not dead.

"Sounds great. Shall we tell my sisters and your friends, or just run away secretly?"

"I'm all for full disclosure. And I can just have my assistant take care of it all so we don't have to deal with any emotional backlash. You know how people tend to take awards and weddings so seriously."

We're both laughing pretty hard now. I keep reminding myself to stay present to how fun this is, in this moment, without projecting how badly it will inevitably end and how much suffering is in store. *This does not have to be another example of failure Monique. You've had plenty of those. Maybe this is the perfect setup for a juicy Vegas affair, or even just a lovely interaction with another human being that is bringing me pleasure. This is enough,* I keep telling myself.

"I am a chef." It comes out of my mouth before I know what I'm saying. Oh boy. Now I've really set us up for a fantasy.

His eyes widen. "Amazing," he says. "Now that's what I call art and science… and magic. I would give any of my buildings to be able to cook something that makes people experience how I feel after a good meal."

"You don't cook?"

"Yes, actually I do. But not very well. My family is Argentinean and Italian - food is everything. It's in our blood, but unfortunately mine is buried a little bit deeper. I do ok, I guess, but nothing like what you must do. I can only imagine what you must create in the kitchen," he says making me immediately think of sex. What is this guy doing to my mind?

Everything he says is seductive. Flamingly seductive. I flash into a scene of us in my kitchen with lots of food and very little clothing. Yum.

"Maybe when we are in Argentina, you will cook something for me." That jolts me out of my reverie, forcing me to remember his joke just minutes before.

"Fair enough I suppose, in exchange for you taking me on a tour of South America to view your buildings."

This is getting so rich and delicious I can hardly stand it.

We spend the rest of the flight talking about our lives, joking about our fantasy trip and comparing Vegas itineraries. We disembark together and head to baggage claim together (even though neither of us checked luggage) and walk outside together.

"Are your sisters picking you up?" he asks.

I laugh. Too loudly perhaps.

"We're not that kind of family. It's all about independence with us. And besides, they are much too busy getting the party started. It's ok. It's such a short taxi ride."

He clears his throat, clearly wanting to say something. "I would love if you came with me. I mean... I have a car. I mean I'm getting picked up... a car service... and we're going to the same place. And you could come."

He stops talking and lowers his head. I can tell he had a hard time with that. The thought of him feeling a bit nervous with me is too ridiculous to believe. I am just this boring mom pretending to be glamorous, living a fake life to go with my fake weekend. He is this gorgeous, most likely brilliant architect with a global business. Did I mention gorgeous? Oh and smart. And really well spoken, with great manners and sweet breath... ok I have to stop.

"Yes, that would be great. If you don't mind." Sexy smile.

"I would love it. But I think I said that already," he chuckles.

I follow him as he strides toward door number 6. I notice, as it is my favorite number. Good sign. A quick glimpse in the reflective glass soothes my worries just a bit. I actually look pretty damn good. At least for me. Things are holding up and those extra sessions at the gym (to work off all my sexual tension) are paying off. Maybe I'm not so far out of his league.

Just outside is a sleek black limo with his name in the window. As he approaches confidently, the driver asks, "Mr. Gonzales?"

"Yes, thank you."

He opens the door for me, and stands there as I enter. I notice him looking at my legs. Good, I think. Very good. We had all inherited those great legs from Mom, whose legs were out of some fashion magazine. Absolutely perfect. Even when I couldn't stand the rest of me, I knew my legs could stand up to scrutiny. No problem to linger there a little bit.

We sit very close to each other in the limo. Closer than strangers normally would.

"You are leaving on Monday right?" He had asked me that already. What is up, I wonder?

"Yes. After we recover from our raucous celebration of Nora's big win. She's convinced that she has no chance but my sister is the golden girl. She works her ass off and wins. A lot. Lizzy and I are both expecting to see her up on stage with a no-tears acceptance speech. She's not one for soft emotions."

"And you? Will you be crying?"

"Most certainly. I'll probably be crying for the other categories and the other winners too. I may even start if we see an especially touching billboard on the way there. Yup. That's me."

"Lovely," he says looking at me so deeply I think he might be reading my mind. It feels as if hours have passed. Or at least minutes. I'm not sure.

"I have to ask you something, Monique."

"Yes?" Curious. So curious.

"Would you have time to go somewhere with me?"

"You mean other than Argentina?"

"Yes. Somewhere local. For now at least." Gosh that smile is going to be the end of me.

"There is a restaurant I have been wanting to try. It is supposed to be spectacular. I would like to take you there, if you have time."

Oh my God, he just asked me out. On a date. Perhaps I misheard. No, it was definitely a date. Shit. What am I going to do? Would the girls understand? I know they are hoping to spend all our time together. But how can I say no to this man? Oh boy...

"That sounds really nice. As long as you understand I love to eat. People have been frightened when taking me out to dinner."

"I can't wait to experience that. I am definitely up for the challenge." The grin again. "Does tomorrow work for you?"

"Actually, could I just check with my sisters? Nora is a real stickler and likes to have everything planned out. I just need to see if Friday or Saturday is better."

As if we were using our sibling ESP, my phone beeps with a message. Nora, I am sure.

Where are you, Nik? Do I really need to be the only one drinking in this family??

"Excuse me," I say to him. "I need to get back to the boss."

On my way. In a shiny black limo. You are welcome to pull yourself off the barstool and greet me at the entrance, like a sister with manners would do.

Limo?? Who are you? And what have you done with my simpleton sister??

I show him the text exchange, which sends him into gales of laughter.

"I see all of you are very funny. I can tell you love each other a lot."

"Yes. Despite outer appearances, we do. And this is the real me... the simpleton sister. Now you know."

"I can't imagine what your family must be like to think you are a simpleton. You are not in the Gabor family, are you?

While you have your phone out, why don't I give you my number so you can let me know about tomorrow? I don't want to intrude on your time with your sisters, really. But I would love to spend some time with you. It has been a wonderful afternoon, talking to you."

I hand him my phone like a star-struck teenager. I even giggle, embarrassingly enough.

He takes it confidently and begins to type in lots of characters. Many more than I would have expected. I hold myself back from peaking over his shoulder but the anticipation is killing me. What the heck is he writing? Does he have one of these extra-long Latin names? Is he writing me a love note? Hee, hee hee. The girlish giggles come out again.

He hands me the phone.

"Ok, I put my full name, so you can find me at the hotel. Also my cell and email. And a little note so you remember who I am."

"Do you think I would forget you?" I am really surprised. Has this guy not looked in the mirror lately?

"I would never presume that I made nearly as much of an impression on you as you made on me."

Humble to top it all. I am toast!

We are mostly silent for the last few minutes of the trip. I like sitting next to him, hearing and feeling his breath. Every now and then we look over at each other and smile. No words needed. Also surprisingly, not awkward.

We arrive and someone from the hotel opens my door. Marco comes around from his side and takes my hand to help me out of the car. I could almost swear that he pushed the valet out of the way. His hand feels sooooooooo nice. Big and warm and not too soft. The hands of a man who used them. Unspeakably sexy.

We stand face to face for the briefest moment and the idea of kissing him crosses my mind. Not something that *regular* me would do in a million years. But the goddess diva? Definitely. The moment passes before I can move on my impulse. Perhaps I will be given another opportunity. Hopefully.

We follow the bellboys, with our luggage, into the hotel and the bustle of Las Vegas. This town is a secret passion of mine. Not something I admit to too many people - it doesn't really match my down-to-earth image - but the part of me that loves glitz and glam and stardom feels at home here. I can't help but grin.

I head towards the unfortunately long check-in line when Marco wraps his arm around my waist and whispers, "Come with me."

We move past the crowds to a desk, off to one side. I think the sign says VIP or concierge or something like that. I'm too busy taking in the sights and sounds of Vegas. Gosh, I'm happy to be here. And not only because this amazing man has his arm around me.

He provides his information, to which the stunning woman behind the counter coos, "Welcome to the Wynn, Mr. Gonzales. So wonderful to have you back." He tells her that I will also be checking in and he would appreciate her help. She obliges.

My sister had reserved us fabulous rooms, certainly, but I'm not sure I would have gotten this level of service. I am very grateful.

He listens closely as she tells me my room number. I notice.

We step away from the desk and pause for a moment, neither of us sure of what to do next. Do we go up to our rooms together? Would he even use the same pedestrian elevator the rest of us use? Do I shake hands, hug, or kiss as the Europeans (and South Americans do)? So confusing.

The problem is solved by the piercing shriek of my baby sister, her tiny yet curvy frame bobbing across the lobby toward me. Right behind, not stooping to excitement, is my equally-pleased older sister. They look fabulous, in full Vegas style.

"You're finally here!!! Oh my God, we were waiting for you for so long." Lizzy keeps talking, even as she wraps her body around mine. "Sooooo glad you're here. Oh my God, Nik, this place is amazing! I might want to live here. It is the BEST EVER," says the soon-to-be mom.

Even Nora gives me a sweet hug. "So glad you're here, Nik," she whispers in my ear. I know she means it.

They barely notice the man waiting patiently next to me. "Hey guys, this is Marco. We flew in together."

"Whaaaaaat???!!!" screeches Lizzy. "You know this guy??? Oh my God!" It was hard to believe that this girl had not been drinking.

"We met in the..."

"Hello. I'm Nora. I'm the reason we're here. And you are?" My sister, always the professional, always the boss.

He takes Nora's hand then pulls her in and kisses both her cheeks. She is kissed into silence. A very rare occurrence.

"I am Marco Gonzales. Your beautiful sister graced me with her presence on what would otherwise have been an uneventful plane ride. I am so pleased to meet you. She described you quite well."

Nora can't speak and neither of us knows what to do. It was unheard of. Lizzy takes this moment of silence to make her introduction, which she does by jumping up for her own hug and kiss. Except that Lizzy is so small and Marco is so tall that she jumps up on him like a small child on her father. He catches her, thankfully, and gracefully puts her down.

We all erupt in laughter that lasts minutes. Lizzy, not one to hold onto embarrassment, happily accepts his two-cheeked kiss.

"Wow, you are so handsome!" she exclaims. I would have turned red if my olive skin didn't hide it so well. "Did you really just meet Nik on the plane? And was it your limo she came in? That is so awesome! I love meeting awesome people on the plane. Did she tell you I'm pregnant? Yup, it's true. At first I was like, oh shit! But now I'm super excited and I feel really good now that all the throwing up is done and my fabulous sisters have offered to help me and Nik is the best mom I have ever met and she's going to teach me how to be the best mom ever and..."

"Lizzy, shall we save some of our life history for later? Marco probably has somewhere he needs to be," the voice of reason chimes in.

"Well, yes and no. I am meeting my friends fairly soon, but it's Vegas, which means that time is flexible. And this is MUCH more interesting." Marco graces them all with the killer smile.

"I am very excited for you, Lizabetta." (Now did he really have to say it in the most sexy and glamorous way???)

"Parenthood is the journey of heroes and holds riches beyond anything you could imagine."

"You have kids?" she asks.

"Yes, two boys although they are nearly men now. Both in college."

I did not know this. I feel awkward about it.

"Cool," she says. "Too bad they're not a teensy bit older, because they are probably HOT!!!"

"Lizzy!!!" I have to intervene this time, but Marco just laughs.

"Yes, I think they are very handsome. And they seem to like slightly older women, so maybe..." He winks.

When Lizzy laughs it is like drinking champagne. So light and effervescent. It's wonderful to see her this happy.

"So, when will we see you again?"

"Lizzy!!!" I think I might just die of embarrassment. Right here in the hotel lobby.

"Funny you should ask. I have invited your sister to dinner with me, and she is wondering when it would be convenient for you to be without her. For a night."

Did he say *A* night, or *THE* night?

"Oh, whenever is fine. We're just hanging out. Other than Nora's thing on Sunday, but that won't take very long."

All Nora or I can do is sigh.

"Good to hear."

Exasperated, Nora says, "Shall we?" as she leads us towards the elevators. Awkwardness fills the space as we wait for one of the doors to open. Lizzy looks like she is trying hard to contain her excitement, and I can't tell what Nora is feeling. I feel strange, a little ashamed of my family but heck, this is the reality of my life.

We get into a packed elevator and Marco makes his way next to me. Our bodies are very close and I can feel myself grow warm. I definitely want this man, if nothing more for than a seriously good romp. Maybe lots more.

He bends down as if to kiss my neck and whispers in my ear, "I apologize for intruding on your schedule. I did not mean to bring it up with your sisters. I know you would have talked to them. I hope you don't think I was too forward."

I can't believe what I am hearing and have to take a breath before responding. And boy, do I like having his face so close to mine.

I turn toward his ear and say, "It's ok. No problem, really. It looks like we are good for tomorrow night."

"That's wonderful."

And then he kisses me. Slowly, lingering, one kiss on each cheek. As he passes my lips I imagine what that would feel like. My arousal raises the temperature in the elevator by several degrees.

I beam back at him as I make my way through the doors onto our floor.

"Call me later, ok?"

"Absolutely," I say.

The three of us get off the elevator and hold our composure until the doors close. We then begin to jump up and down like lottery winners. We can hardly make it to the room before we completely let loose.

"Nik, that man is unbelievable. Oh my God you have to do him. You have to. He probably has an amazing body too." Lizzy is the most sexual of the three of us and pregnancy does not appear to be slowing her down.

"He is very charming, Nik. Well done. I approve," the boss adds. Marco seems to have infiltrated Nora's typical skepticism.

"Well now, I feel so much better because I was like, eh, about the whole thing." The screaming begins again.

"This is going to be the weekend to end all weekends, girls!!"

"Yes, Lizzy, I think you're right," I have to add. "And you, the reason why we're here. Anything to say?"

"I'm glad you guys came. It's been too long since we did this."

"Don't get soft on us, girl!" says Lizzy.

They give me a tour of our adjoining rooms, with mine in the middle. With all the interior doors open, we have a huge great space, but decide that my room will be party central. I am happy to oblige.

"Can a girl get something to eat around here? I have to take care of some serious pent-up sexual energy!!"

"Yes, yes, let's eat! You know I'm always up for that. Where should we go?" asks Lizzy.

"Nik, we've got this great fruit and cheese spread here. Would that work? Then we can get ready and go out for the night a little later?" My sister, the planner, always has the most logical solution.

"What are you guys going to wear? I'm going to get ready for our big night. Music! We need music!" Lizzy is already dancing around, even before the music starts.

Lizzy and Nora provide the soundtrack for our preparations, complete with singing, drumming on the furniture and a few rounds of the hustle. I haven't felt this happy and alive and... like a woman... in so long.

I prepare outfit number one for the weekend. Understatedly sexy. Well, maybe not so understated.

Inspired by the dance party, we get dressed and strut out of the rooms as if Vegas is our own personal runway. There are yards of legs on display, each of us knowing which asset to feature. Lizzy's chosen a flouncy skirt and, in acknowledgment of her pregnancy-inspired bust-line, a low cut top. The baby bump is hardly visible.

Nora wears a leather pencil skirt to accentuate her slimness and nonstop legs. I wear shorts. Silver glitter shorts that Claire (my resident fashion diva) forced me to buy but that I never expected to wear in public. Where else but Vegas?

I remember Mom and her short skirts. Even as she got older (not that she actually aged), she knew exactly what she was going to feature on her body and wasn't shy about it.

Crossing the casino, I can see the heads turn, and the eyes watching us. It feels spectacular. To be desired again is like the first breath after being underwater. This is what it feels like to be alive, I realize.

Is that my name I hear? No, couldn't be. Then again. We all stop and Lizzy sees him first. "Marco! It's Marco!" she says excitedly.

I turn around to see an outline of a man straight from his own runway. Royal blue cashmere sweater and dark jeans. I think Lizzy is right, this man has an amazing body, much more apparent now that he isn't in the suit he was wearing earlier. I really have to play it cool here, even though I want to swoon. He walks directly to me and I go straight in. First to one cheek, and then slowly to the other. I give his arm a squeeze and confirm everything I believe to be underneath that silky soft sweater. We are frozen in space, just the two of us, my happily hopping sister aside.

"Well, hello," I say.

"Ladies." Long pause. "You have made it impossible for any of these other poor women who have worked so hard, to get any male attention." He turns to Lizzy first, who is dying for her double cheek kisses. "You have forever redefined what an expectant mother looks like. I hope you never worry about being sexy, my dear."

She beams at him, as if he had read her mind about a big part of her anxiety about pregnancy.

Nora is next.

"And you. The serious Nora with the mile-long legs. I can see why you need all that seriousness to contain those legs. They are lethal."

Once again, Nora is silenced. This is good.

I realize he's been holding my hand the whole time. He turns to me and kisses my hand, ever so softly. He doesn't speak and I think maybe he has nothing to say. I am starting to feel a bit embarrassed and unsure about my garish outfit choice.

"Come meet my friends. I'm not sure I can let you out of my sight tonight. You outshine the whole Vegas strip." His gaze never wavers from my eyes.

I would have followed him anywhere he lead me at that point. Without saying anything more, we head towards a lounge across the casino. I don't know how he spotted me from there, with all these people around. Vegas is never short of eye candy and I am so glad he found me.

"Monique is hungry! She needs to eat!" Lizzy adds. Oh yeah, I have completely forgotten. The apple was delicious, but my body is asking for real food. Among other things.

"Well, may I feed you then?"

Everything in my body is saying yes. Feed me, consume me, anything you want.

We walk through a busy collection of bodies, hand in hand. I am unsure where he is leading us, and am surprised when he walks into a room that you couldn't tell existed from the front of the lounge. It grows surprisingly quiet.

This is clearly some VIP area, with a much more subdued feel than the rest of the place. It is beautiful, sexy, elegant. Just like him.

With our hands still clasped, he leads me and my sisters up to a group of men, who stop as if on cue. They can't tell which of us to look at first. They are impressed. I am pleased.

It could have been a Latin supermodel convention, each man better looking than the next. Please join us, says the young one in black. I can see Lizzy's eyes get wide. He is definitely her type.

"Amigos, this is Monique." A nod of recognition goes through the group. Had he told them about me? "And her sisters, Lizabetta and Nora." They each in turn get up to kiss us and introduce themselves. This ritual is really growing on me.

I look back to see if Nora is ok with this change of plans. She had a restaurant in mind that she wanted to try and Nora did not like to deviate from the plan.

When our eyes meet, she smiles and I can tell it is fine.

"They serve food here right? Nik is hungry!"

I love how Lizzy is always looking out for us in just the sweetest way. She is going to make a great mom.

The men make room for us to join in and the party begins. I don't know who is ordering the food and drinks but everything just keeps coming. Marco never lets our bodies get more than a foot away from each other. His hands remain around my waist, on my back or holding mine. I feel like a queen. A very sexy queen.

Hours pass and no one makes a move to leave. The conversations are flowing with Nora showing off her Spanish and talking about her time in South America. They regale her with stories of each of their homelands and make her promise to visit. Lizzy and her young man create their own dance floor and practice the salsa or the rumba. I can't tell.

Marco and I float in our private bubble, speaking with our faces inches away, about life and food and buildings and beauty. I start to feel like I could love this man. What isn't there to love?

Somehow we agree to move the party to the dance club. The groom's brother has gotten VIP passes and there is apparently Latin music in one of the rooms.

Moving back out into the fray is a shock but Marco glues his body to mine. The crush of bodies trying to get into the club almost separates us, but the men created a protective wall. I am being completely protected and taken care of. This fantasy of a night just keeps getting better.

The pulse of the music hits my body well before we enter the club and I want to move. My sisters are the singers of the family, but I am the dancer. I feel music in my hips and my back and my legs and can express it well. I am already moving when Marco pulls me to the dance floor. "Let's see what you can do, my chef."

My chef. He said my chef. I don't think anyone has ever called me *their* chef. The implications are too much to contemplate. Now, I just need to move. He is surprised that I can follow him, but I do. We go from a close embrace Latin-style to freeform dance and back again. My body is free, taken by the music.

Dance is how our ancestors judged each other's physical suitability for mating, and the same thing is happening here. I can feel him, and he can feel me. There is mutual appreciation and I keep having visions of being naked with him. Would he be a good lover? Would it even go that far?

At several points he reaches down to whisper something in my ear. Every time his face comes close to mine, I give a start. There is undeniable electricity there.

Occasionally, I remember my sisters, and have a look around the club. We have deviated pretty seriously from the plan, and I want to make sure they are ok. As far as I can tell, they are both having fun.

"I have to ask you something," he says fairly seriously. I feel nervousness begin to flood my body. Will this be the proposition? Or the dump? *Stop projecting, Monique, just enjoy the moment,* I keep telling myself. He leads me into a quieter part of the club, where we can hear each other a bit better.

"I don't know quite how to say this."

Uh-oh is all I hear in my head.

"I know you are here for your sisters. But I don't really know why you are here. I mean, I don't know if you wanted to meet some... people and have fun. I mean of course you wanted to have fun. That was stupid to say."

He is the one who is nervous. What is going on for him?

"What I'm trying to say is that, I don't know if you want this. All this time with me. I feel like maybe I am keeping you from something."

Was he worried about my looking around the room for my sisters? Did he feel my nervousness and think it was lack of interest? I need to be powerful here. "What do you want to know, Marco?" All of a sudden, I become the cool one. Calm, collected, expressive. The power of it all is nearly ecstatic.

"Yes, the question," he says nodding. "I want to know if you want to be with me. I mean, if it's ok that I am keeping you here. I just... We are having so much fun, and I would like to spend this time with you, but not force you, if you don't want."

"Does it look like I don't want?" Power is a dangerous thing and now I am playing with him. This is my MO, to take advantage of men when they are being vulnerable with me. To attack when they are defenseless. I am disgusted that this is coming out now, with this man.

Before I can retract the question, he answers. "I think you are enjoying yourself," he says strongly. "And so are your sisters. But Vegas is a funny place. Sometimes... it can be easy to misread things and I don't want to do that. I want to be clear."

"Yes, me too. I am here to enjoy myself, in whatever form that takes. And if I wasn't, I wouldn't still be here."

"That is very clear."

A moment of awkward silence is broken when I touch his arm. I want to tell him that I am completely in awe of his directness and his consideration. That the whole power trip is a pretense. That I feel thrilled and terrified in his presence. I can't quite muster the courage for that.

"I'm going to the bathroom. Be right back."

"Ok."

I take extra time in the bathroom to review what just happened. He's right. It's so easy to misread and misunderstand. I had done it quite enough times in my life. Part of me is terrified about how I already feel about him, after just a few hours together. And the other part hears what I said - *I am here to enjoy myself. In whatever form that takes.* And desperately want to believe it.

Marco is talking to a friend when I come out. Spanish is flying between their lips and I struggle to understand what is being said.
   Damn! I wish I had paid more attention in Spanish class!

"Hola Bella," he says as he takes my hand and kisses it.

"Everything ok?" I ask, expecting to hear otherwise.

"Of course. Except that we are here and the music is out there. Shall we?"

"Absolutely."

Any tentativeness he has about our being together is lost, which he shows me on the dance floor. He holds my body so close to his that sometimes I can't breathe. I think I can feel him hard, through his pants, but convince myself it couldn't possibly be, even though we are dancing as if we are making love. Our bodies are filled with fire and spark; I'm certain he can feel the music through my own pulse. His hands explore me, and I like it. Nearly as much as my hands on his body.

I want him to kiss me so badly. My mouth aches for his. But he doesn't. What does this man want, and will I be able to give it to him?

The way we move together definitely bodes well for anything that might happen further along. This man can really move, and more importantly he can move with me. He is a very strong leader, and I let myself surrender to him. It is delicious.

And sexy and magical and so erotic. Even if nothing happens between us, I will look back at this night and know I had a hot moment with a hot guy. And had a great time.

I lose myself in those moments with him so many times that I completely lose track of time. It's only when Lizzy finds me to say she needs to eat that I realize it is morning. No windows in Vegas mean morning and night are indistinguishable.

Lizzy's handsome friend offers to take her to breakfast but I'm not sure she wants to be alone with him. Normally she would have been the first person to leave with a guy, but pregnancy has made her a bit more skittish. And sensitive maybe. And sensible certainly.

Thankfully, Marco makes the decision.

"I'm hungry too. Your wild sister kept me dancing all night with no sustenance. Can we accompany you to breakfast?"

"Yes! That's great!" says my always enthusiastic Lizzy.

Before the four of us head out, I remember Nora.

"Where's Nora?"

"She's still out there," says Lizzy. "Said she didn't want to eat. She's in the middle of a group of men, doing her snake dance."

This is what we call Nora's dancing. She is so tall and skinny and doesn't really have rhythm but does this slithery sinewy movement that seems to mesmerize everyone around her. She loves being the center of attention, and I know she is having fun.

We decide on the German pancake house, which tickles Lizzy to no end, but it is a cab ride away, which means we have to go outside into the light of day. I am terrified about what I must look like after so many hours of dancing. Hard. Maybe this isn't a good idea. But it is too late and I am being lead along.

I don't realize how hungry I am until I see the food around us. This is a superbly good choice and we all eat until we are almost sick. These amazing pancakes, several inches thick but light and delicious, are probably meant for Bavarian lumberjacks, but we devour them. Marco watches me eat as if he is studying a piece of art, grinning at my exuberant enjoyment.

"I need to eat many meals with you Monique. It makes everything more delicious."

My fork stops midway to my mouth as I contemplate where I want his mouth to be.

We are all hitting a wall now. At least I am. It's time to call it a night. Or a morning as the case may be.

We begin to make the trek back to the hotel, and at one point I fall asleep on Marco's shoulder. I awake as he kisses my forehead.

"Time to go, Bella." I like that he calls me that, cheesy as it might be. We hold hands all the way down the hallway to my room and Lizzy's, hardly speaking. Will he make a move, I keep thinking? Will I invite him in? It is all so unclear, the long night and the events of the day creating quite a blur in my mind.

Maybe tonight is not the night, I think. I am so sweaty. But so is he. Would showering together be out of the question? What I really want is to just sleep with him, really just sleep. But no, it's too soon for that, I rationalize.

All four of us stop at Lizzy's door. It is awkward. Marco probably knows his friend will make a move and wants to give him some privacy. What can we do? My room is only next door, not enough space for us to be inconspicuous. Wow, this is weird, a flashback to my teen years.

"Come with me," he says. I am exhausted, but I follow him anyway, back into the elevator, to the very top of the hotel. He has a penthouse, I realize. Holy shit. He is taking me up to his room. Am I ready? Am I willing? I try to summon my good decision-making skills right there, but can't. I follow my body, which wants his body, right into his room.

I am aghast at the view. The entire Las Vegas strip is laid out in front of me through floor-to-ceiling windows. It is spectacular. I put my hands on the cool glass, mesmerized, and stare out. He goes into the kitchen and comes back with two glasses of water.

What a thoughtful guy. He just doesn't quit.

"I didn't mean to rush you in here," he says sheepishly. "I just didn't know what to do because Esteban and Liz..."

"Yes, I understand. It is so beautiful up here. I can't imagine how you got this room."

"Aaaahhh. It's Esteban. He is a high roller here. Brings lots of clients who pay big money. And we are having the wedding here, so they gave us this whole floor. It is beautiful, though, isn't it?"

"Yes," is all I can say.

"You are very tired," he says turning me to look in my eyes.

"Yes." Again just yes.

"Please let me know when you want me to walk you back to your room. I imagine they have made some decision by now." We both snicker, then I remember...

"Doesn't he mind that she's pregnant?" I don't know where that came from.

Marco laughs. "Well, it's actually quite funny. Esteban is younger than me. Youngest in the group and the first one to want children. More than any man I have ever known, this man wants children. Lots of them. I think he saw her, and she is very beautiful, of course, and when he saw that she was pregnant... well, I think he fell in love instantly.

A bit like when I saw you daydreaming at the airport. A woman who could dream things that make her face light up like that must have magic in her soul."

I want to be more wide awake to process what I am hearing. Did he really just say...

"Are you thinking of those things now?" he inquires.

"No. There are other things now. Maybe even better things."

He likes that answer and takes my face in his hands.

"This face... this magnificent face. How has any man managed to let you go?"

"Well, some quite easily," I joke. I feel the moment getting more serious than I am capable of handling.

"Foolish." And he moves toward me, still holding my face. My breath quickens. He is so close to me. Just one more inch and our lips will touch, but he stays there. Just outside me. I think I will dissolve or catch on fire or both at the same time. This is too much. Is he now playing with me?

So slowly that I barely know he has moved I feel his warm mouth on mine. He holds me there as his kiss grows firmer. His lips part mine and next we are devouring each other. My God, I want to consume this man, I want to take him into every part of me.

He kisses me strongly and then backs away, in a rhythm I can instantly understand. Just like our dance, he is constantly reading my body, my breath, my mouth. My fatigue begins to slip away as he takes me further and further into him.

"Marco..." I breathe into his mouth.

"I have been waiting all day for that," he says. "It was well worth it."

My eyes stay closed to take in what he is saying but I find his mouth again. And now my hands begin to explore his body. All the curves and angles of his bones and muscles feel like something surreal.

As he moves to my neck, I fall under the tidal wave of my desire. This man ignites me. He listens and pays attention and always figures out exactly what to do. I moan aloud, despite myself. He responds with his own groan.

His hands grasp my buttocks, pulling me towards him and now there is no doubt what I am feeling. He is fully aroused and wants me to know. He finds the skin beneath my blouse and the sensation of flesh on flesh shocks me. He stops, unsure of whether I am signaling him to stop. I assure him with my mouth that all is fine. Better than fine.

"Stay with me," he whispers. I'm not sure I hear him, and move just far enough away to look directly into his face.

"Stay with me," he repeats, now stronger. Our faces are apart, but he never stops holding me tightly against him. "I don't expect anything from you, I just want you to stay with me tonight."

"Today." I am disgusted with my unnecessary need to clarify and correct. My inexperience and clumsiness are starting to show.

"Yes. Today. Right now."

He waits for my answer, and I try to find one. I desperately want to stay with him. I want to rip his clothes off and fuck him like there is no tomorrow. I want to scream and writhe in ecstasy.

"Not tonight," I say instead, unsure of why those words come out of my mouth.

He is disappointed, but not surprised.

"I promise you, I don't expect anything. I'm just not ready to let you go yet."

I consider his promise, and realize I believe him. I think I can stay there, and not have sex with him. It would be delightful to be held by this man while I fall asleep.

"I...I..." Nothing. I can't find an answer.

"You are worried about something. Can I ease your worries somehow?"

"I don't know. I would love to stay with you, but..."

"You are not comfortable. Yet. I understand. You don't know me." He is nodding, convincing himself more than anything else, I believe.

"Maybe I should go." I don't want to go. Please convince me to stay!

"As you wish, Bella. Let's go down."

We walk hand in hand all the way to my door, in silence. What is there to say? Did I just totally blow this opportunity? Would I get another one?

"I really look forward to seeing you tonight. Just us, right?"

"Right. Good night, Marco. Thank you for a wonderful evening. I had a great time."

He moves toward me, perhaps with the intention of a gentle kiss goodnight, but the energy catches me and I respond passionately. I pull him in this time, with insistence. I want him to understand that my decision does not reflect my current state of desire. Or my feelings for him (God help me!).

My back is against the door and our bodies are grinding. My body is changing my mind. All I have to do is open the door and we will fall into my bed and there will be no more false no's, no more insecurity, no more ridiculous restraint.

But he pulls away first, this time. Did he feel my resolve fading?

"Good night, Bella. I can't wait to see you again."

Though my mouth must be open, I can't say anything as he walks away.

I enter my room in a daze. Did all of this really happen?

Knock, knock. Is he at the door? I get excited. No, it's the internal door. It's Lizzy.

"Are you up? Let me in!"

I open the door to my baby sister, not hopping so much but grinning from ear to ear.

"I can't believe you didn't stay with him. What happened? Ok you have to tell me everything. I have to say the two of you are the hottest couple I have ever seen. More sex appeal and chemistry than Brad and Angelina. Seriously. It was so hot to watch you – he's a seriously good dancer too. So why didn't you stay? Did something weird happen?"

I know that Lizzy will just continue talking unless I stop her.

"Nothing happened. I just really like this guy. I mean **really** and I sort of... panicked. Maybe he's not a one-night kind of guy. Maybe I should wait and make it... important. Maybe I'm just full of shit and scared. It's been a while for me, you know."

"Of course I know! Which is why you should have totally jumped his bones!"

"Who says that? What are we, 12?"

Lizzy gets into my bed.

"Well, make yourself comfortable."

"Oh, come on. You know you want to snuggle. The baby wants her favorite auntie to stay with her."

How can I resist?

"I want to hear about your young man. There were some serious sparks, baby girl!"

My baby sister and I, and her baby, all crawl into bed late in the morning after a wild night in Vegas and sleep. Like babies.

6

WANTING AND HAVING

The next thing I hear is a knock followed by the unmistakable voice of my sister.

"Rise and shine you lazy-bones."

I swear Nora is not human. Part alien, part sea creature, part robot. Seriously. She strides into the room as if she has just spent the last few hours in a salon. Lizzy buries herself further under the blankets, with a slight groan.

Without opening my eyes I ask, "Why do you even knock, if you're just going to come in anyway?" I can't hide the bitterness in my voice. What could be so important that we needed to be awoken?

"Listen, we need to nail down the agenda for today. There are a lot of moving parts. I've got some important meetings this afternoon, Lizzy, you've got all the spa appointments and Nik, well, I'm not sure if the plan to do some chef schmoozing has been superseded by getting laid. You'll have to sort that one out yourself."

"Fuck you," I barely have the energy to say.

"In any case, I'll be expecting to see you all at 6pm tonight, which is really not that many hours from now. And I expect you to be looking fabulous, relatively of course. These are important people to meet and I am serious about being impressive. Got it?"

"Nik can't make it," groans the voice under the covers. I love my baby sis, always looking out for me. I give her an extra squeeze for remembering my date, which I had nearly forgotten. "She's got dinner with the Latin hottie. Remember? We all agreed. Or was I the only sober one?"

Nora sighs in exasperation. "Ok, I really am interested in what's happening with you two. It all looks excessively interesting. I just want to make sure you guys know what I expect."

"Stop acting like our mother, Nora. She wasn't even like this. We're here for fun, remember?" Lizzy is getting angry.

I can see this is going to escalate.

"Don't worry Nora. We will be there," I reassure her. "I will be there to meet and greet, then I'm off with Marco. We are here for you. We know this is a big deal. Ok?"

"Ok." She really wants to pout and continue making her point but doesn't have the basis for complaint. Sometimes it's quite helpful that she has that scientific mind. Logic rules.

Lizzy peeks her head out to make sure everyone is ok.

"Ok sleepyheads. Can't wait to hear about your Latin lovers. Have a great day and I'll see you later. Love you."

"Love you too Nona," we say at the same time, using our childhood pet name for her. "Knock 'em dead Dr. Bad-ass!"

I realize going back to sleep isn't going to be an option for me, no matter how bleary I feel.

"I want to get some sun. How about you, baby girl?"

"Sleep. Just me and this bed. Maybe some room service and massage. Mmmmmmmmm..."

"Sounds lovely. I'm going to check out the pool and I'll see you back in time to get ready. Love you sweet girl." I give her a big hug, kiss and belly rub.

The first look in the mirror is a bit of a shocker. It is going to take some major work to get things back to a presentable state. At my age, a long night out makes itself very apparent: dark circles, splotches, immovable makeup remnants. The work begins.

A bit of breakfast, or lunch, will do me good. I didn't drink that much, thankfully, but not enough rest leaves me ravenous. Even after that pancake fest we just enjoyed a few hours before.

I'm in the bathroom when I hear more knocks. Did Nora really need to check on us again? Goodness gracious! But then another round of knocks. This is not Nora. Housekeeping maybe? I forgot to hang the Do Not Disturb sign. I can hear Lizzy muttering under the blankets.

I open the door just a crack, prepared to ask them to come back later, when I see the beautifully set table.

"Room service," says the cheery older man. Confusion keeps me silent for a beat. "We didn't order room service," I say quizzically.

"Yes, ma'am. It was ordered for you. A nice gift." His smile broadens.

Nora, I think, ensuring our rising promptly and being in decent shape for her event later. Nice, I suppose, if it wasn't so damn controlling.

"From Nora," I ask, knowing the answer. He shakes his head. Perhaps he doesn't understand what I'm saying.

"No ma'am. This is from..." he pauses to take out the sheet of paper to make sure he is getting it right. "It's from Mr. Gonzales in the penthouse. Will you accept?"

Surprise silences me for a moment, but I move my body away from the door enough for him to enter. I point to the bed and make a sound of shushing.

He nods and smiles, then quietly sets up the beautiful brunch Marco had sent for me, complete with a magnificent bouquet. I feel myself flush at the memory of our last few moments together. It could so easily have ended with us together, fully together, and didn't. Still he sends me this amazing gift. Part of me wants to discover what I'm missing. What is the trick? How can this situation keep proving itself too good to be true?

Everything is scrumptious, clearly hand selected. I can tell he really thought of my tastes. Part of me wants to run upstairs and thank him. With my body. Then I realize I can't even get up there anyway, as it requires a special key.

Ok, don't get ahead of yourself, I think. The day is young, and you need something in your system. I finish eating, while Lizzy sleeps, convincing myself a bit of distraction from this man will do me good. I'm worried about how obsessive I am feeling, and decide to be content in this quiet moment. Or pretend to be content.

Vegas-ready swimsuit on, I make my way down to the pool, which in true Vegas style, looks more like an outdoor nightclub than swimming spot. The music is pumping, the drinks are flowing and all the beautiful Vegas-ites are continuing the party.

By sheer luck, I happen to see a group leaving and score one of their lounge chairs. Perfect, I think. Absolutely perfect.

I begin to feel conspicuously alone, and start fidgeting with my phone. Maybe I should send him a quick thank-you note. For brunch. That would be the polite thing to do, certainly, ulterior motives aside.

I look up his number and see the note he had written me the first day we met - yesterday:

Looking forward to our trip to Argentina.

Wow, this guy really has a hold on me. I can feel the energy in my body as I think about him. The memory of his hands on my face, and his lips finding mine, keeps replaying itself in my head. It's making everything just a little bit warmer than even this hot desert day.

I begin to type: *Brunch was a wonderful surprise. Much like you have been.* (Wow. A bit provocative, if I do say so myself.) *Deepest thanks for your thoughtfulness. When Lizzy wakes up I'm sure she will also thank you.* Smiley face. Send.

My body is shaking. Actually shaking. What do I expect, that my text will magically summon him and he will appear before me, ready to pick up where we left off? I never read romance novels, but somehow those fantastical relationship ideas keep filling my imaginings.

Alright, I said thank you. I reached out. Did my part. Now I should just sit back and enjoy this beautiful day. I am about to take a magazine from my bag when my phone dings.

Oh boy. It's probably him. Nervous as anything I turn the phone over to see what he said. I appreciate his prompt response in any case.

Where are you?

Funny. Direct. Ok, I'll play along.

At the pool. Watching the beautiful people do their thing.

You must mean BEING the beautiful people. Excellent.

Not quite sure how to respond to that. Thank you? Maybe some modest phrase? I stare at the message as if it is in another language. Am I supposed to ask him his whereabouts in return? Isn't that a bit too intrusive? But he did it, so maybe that is ok. I sit there pondering the rules of communication and appropriate behavior for minutes. I begin responses then erase them, finding them too provocative or serious or ridiculous. It amazes me how much time I can spend analyzing just a few words...

"Excuse me, ma'am? Here is your champagne." A Vegas-style, scantily clad server appears before me. She is a knockout. Wow.

"No, I'm sorry I didn't order this." She is holding two glasses anyway and I am clearly by myself.

"Hmmmm..." she wonders. "Um, Ms. Malone, right?"

Now she has my attention.

"How did you know my name?"

"That gentleman, by the bar, sent them over for you." And there, of course, is Marco, grinning from ear to ear. I think he enjoys these surprises too much - finding me across a crowded casino, sending me brunch and now my favorite beverage. A girl could get used to this.

His linen shirt opens as he walks towards me, and I see just enough to keep me from actually breathing. I had seen him in a suit, jeans, and now swimwear, and he just keeps getting better looking.

"You are everywhere, my friend," I laugh and shake my head at him.

"If only that were true." Were we both thinking about our separate sleeping arrangements last night? He bends down to kiss me, and I expect to offer my cheeks but he catches my mouth. I think we're both surprised, but linger there. Everything from last night comes bubbling to the surface again. Daylight and a change of scenery haven't dimmed this fire.

"How are you today?" he asks.

"Doing pretty well, considering…"

"I would say you are doing quite well, just from external evidence. May I join you?"

"Of course, but I consider both of those glasses for me, so you'll have to get your own."

"As you wish," he says, with that smile that makes me want to rip my clothes off.

"I'm going to start to think you've secretly embedded a locator chip in my arm, or something. Your ability to find me in the most unlikely places is quite impressive."

"We are like magnets, Bella. Can't you feel it? It is inevitable that I find you."

All I can do is take a slow sip from my glass, and avoid his gaze. This is too much.

He helps me with a change of topic. "Are you swimming, or just laying here being gorgeous?"

"Actually, I was planning on reading a bit. Maybe having a bit of a catnap. It is Vegas after all. All about pleasure."

This makes him laugh. "Yes, pleasure. What a thing to pursue."

"I'm not sure what to say to that Marco. Are we making a point?" I can't hide the defensiveness about last night's events, or non-events.

"No point, Bella." He returns my look with a huge grin, not saying anything more. I'm sure he is thinking what a nut-job I must be.

"I'm not sure if you're attached to this particular spot, but we have a private cabana just behind the bar, if you are interested."

"I would love to," I say graciously. He picks up the glasses, offers me his arm, then wraps the other one around my waist and holds me for a moment before moving. When he kisses me again, ever so lightly, a shiver runs down my spine that nearly sets me down on my ass. But there he is, holding me up in his strong arms.

He leads me to a much more private area, with its own pool. A wonderful piece of sun and shade and civil behavior. I can see a few of the guys from last night spread out on their own loungers.

We sit on the largest one, the size of a bed, and make ourselves comfortable. It is downright sexy.

"Are you swimming, Marco?"

"Yes, I did already. The water is very nice."

"So, you were already here when I texted you?"

"Right here, thinking about you."

"But you don't look wet." Ok that sounds very strange. Can't take it back now.

As he takes his shirt off, I can't believe it is even better than the initial view I had gotten. He is sculpted and bronzed and flawless. I desperately want something to be wrong with this man. Otherwise, I have no chance.

He rubs his hands along his arms and chest, and I immediately flash to something pornographic.

"I suppose you're right. I have dried off. Which means it's time for another dip."

He pulls me up again, right after I chug down the rest of my glass of champagne. I am about to be in front of this god of a man in my swimsuit. Heaven help me.

I peel my dress off slowly, trying to be as seductive as possible, while feeling as awkward as I can imagine. A schoolgirl trying to be a seductress. The story of my life.

As soon as my dress is off, I pull him toward the pool, trying to conceal myself underwater as quickly as possible. He is right. It is wonderfully refreshing. And quiet enough that it feels tranquil.

I begin to float on my back and feel his hands underneath me, holding me up and moving me through the water. It is delightful to feel him touching me, without the hot urgency of desire. It is still there, certainly, but muted by the cool lapping of water on my flesh.

Occasionally he bends me around his body, holding me close to him, like a baby. I stroke his body gently, enjoying the opportunity to experience him this way. I am tall enough rarely to feel small with a man, but in his arms I am completely contained.

"I am very grateful for this pool right now," he says after we've been floating around for a few minutes.

I can't help giving him a quizzical look.

"I get to enjoy you, with my eyes and my hands, while we're both wearing very little."

He is grinning but all I want is to sink to the bottom of the pool. He notices.

"You are so... what is the word? Inscrutable. Sometimes you are so confident and commanding, and sometimes I feel you are like a little girl - shy and nervous."

"I'm not sure inscrutable is the right word." There I go again with my pathological need to correct. What can I say to vault over that gaff? "Isn't that like all women?"

"No, Bella. You are not like any woman I have ever known. I am so intrigued by you."

He pauses and I can see him forming a thought.

"You are very charming. And mysterious. And of course, strikingly beautiful. It makes me want to study you, like a piece of art."

"I'm not sure I want to be studied like that. Seems very impersonal."

"Maybe like a meal, then. Which I would consume. With pleasure."

It takes everything I have to maintain my composure, which I'm not sure I do successfully.

"You are very smooth, Marco. You say these things... they are unbelievable."

"Aaah, do you not believe me?"

I can't look at him. "I don't know what to believe."

He begins to brush his lips against my shoulder. I shiver in the warm water.

The smallest move of his hand, and my top would be off. I could slide my hands down his shorts, and he could take me, right there, in view of all of Las Vegas. I want to scream: Take me! Love me! Right now! I believe you with all my heart!

Instead, I say nothing.

"So it is my job to make you believe."

I desperately want to move to a neutral topic. "Tell me something about your life, Marco."

He smiles with a look that tells me he knows I am uncomfortable with the intensity of the conversation. He abides anyway.

"What would you like to know, Bella?"

"Anything you want to tell me."

"We'll start at the beginning. I was born in Buenos Aires, the oldest of 3 children. My father is Argentinian and my mother was Italian. They met when they were young, both students."

"How did they meet?"

"My father had gone to Italy to study architecture. Actually, I think he was studying women, but that's another story. My mother was working in a gallery, studying painting, when they met. He says he went in to ask for directions, and he left with the love of his life. It's all very romantic, you know."

His eyes are sparkling with mischief and I just want to keep looking at him.

"The story is that he whisked her away to Argentina, despite her parents' refusal. My grandparents always denied all of that. They claim that they gave their absolute blessing."

"Were they happy?"

"Yes, they were very happy. My father got more and more successful and my mother got to live a life as an artist and a mother, which is what she always wanted."

"I mean together. Were they happy together?"

"Yes. But it was a different time. Every man in Argentina had mistresses. And he was no exception."

"How did you feel about that?"

He is clearly uncomfortable. Maybe I'm asking him to reveal too much.

"I know it's not right. But I don't think we can judge other people's relationships. They were better together than most couples I've seen in my life."

I want to stop myself, but I can't. "How do you feel about fidelity?"

"I think it's hard. And not necessarily natural. It's tempting to get what you want whenever you want it. But I think that is the price you pay for... love. That sometimes you sacrifice what you want in order to get what you need."

I am a bit stunned by that answer, unsure whether I agree or not.

"How do *you* feel about fidelity?" he asks me.

I want to get this right. "It's hard enough for me to share myself with one person. More than one at a time is out of the question."

He laughs and I realize what I said was funny. It was not intended that way. I slide myself out of his arms and submerge myself in the water. I need a break.

He is floating when I rise out from underwater. I just want to watch him, stretched out in all his glory, but he stands up as soon as he sees me.

"Would you like to go sit down for a while?" he asks.

"Yes, that sounds like a great idea."

He holds my hand the short walk over to the lounge area. I love how physically attentive he is to me. I try to think about the quality that most impresses me and it lies in the mixture of tenderness and courage. He has been fearless in showing me his interest, without being aggressive. Whatever he's doing, it's working.

I lie down first on the lounger, leaving him plenty of room to spread out, but he brings his body right up to mine. The view of the cloudless sky is wonderful, but I turn on my side to get a better view of the man next to me.

"Tell me about your siblings," I ask.

"My sister lives near my father, still, outside of Buenos Aires. She is the baby, but I feel like she has been taking care of us her whole life. She is a natural mother – which is good, as she has 5 kids. We are very close.

My brother lives in Milan, near where my mother lived. He is a designer. For fashion. Quite good actually. But a bit like a child. Always so competitive, with me and the world. Never got married or settled down. Just enjoying himself with all the models."

"Sounds like that trait runs in your family." I realize how rude that must have sounded and I regret it immediately.

He doesn't respond.

"I'm sorry for saying that. I guess I'm a bit sensitive about men cheating. I didn't mean to offend you."

"Did your husband cheat on you?"

"Yes. Many men have. My history is fairly… sordid."

"I'm sorry to hear that. It surprises me. You are so amazing, Monique. What could these men have wanted that you did not give them?"

"Aaaaah… that would be quite a long list, I believe. I've made many mistakes, Marco. And behaved quite badly on many occasions. I tend to withdraw, or shut down, if I feel threatened. This is not conducive to a loving, trusting relationship, apparently."

It is unclear where this level of honesty is coming from. It is not my typical way.

"Do you feel uncomfortable talking about this?"

"Yes, a little bit. Maybe a lot."

He puts his hand on my cheek and holds it there for a moment before bringing his face to mine. Feeling his warm mouth gives me the goosebumps.

"You seem so open to me, Monique. I can't imagine you being withdrawn. Maybe you chose the wrong men."

"Perhaps. But I was the common denominator. Somehow I got in my head that men are not to be trusted. Which is strange because the two most important me in my life – my father and brother – were the most trustworthy people I've ever known."

"Were your parents happy?"

"They had a fairy tale romance. I've never seen anything like it. They met on the beach in the islands and fell in love at first sight. They even died together."

"I'm so sorry, Bella. How terrible for the rest of you."

"Yes, I can't say I'm fully recovered from that. My brother died shortly before them, so I feel this huge gaping hole where my family used to be. At least I have my sisters. They are my lifesavers."

He doesn't stop looking at me, but I have to avert my eyes. I feel the tears begin to build at the bottom of my throat.

Something a bit less sharp needs to cut the emotion.

"Even Jeff, my evil ex-husband, was supportive about my family!" I am only mostly kidding.

"I guess you don't have the best relationship."

"Actually, we do now. But it was very bad. For very long."

"How long have you been divorced?"

"About three years now, but we had started living separate lives years before that. It was very messy and slightly complicated."

"Will you tell me about it?"

"Are you sure you're ready?"

"I'm absolutely ready, Monique."

That statement sends chills down my spine.

"But first," he continues, "can you lay right here, on my arm?"

Marco stretches his right arm toward me, and taps the area of his chest just below his shoulder. I am happy to slide my head into that most wonderful resting spot.

"Are you sure you won't get too hot?"

"Monique, Bella, it's hot whenever you're around. That's how that works."

I flush, knowing how hot I feel with him. I take a deep breath of his scent and my body tingles.

"We were kind of a strange couple, well suited in so many ways, but never this grand love affair. It just made logical sense for us to be together. I was hypnotized by how powerful and sure of himself he was and I think he saw me as a unique possession to go with his other possessions. He had plotted out our whole lives, he liked things to be well thought out and predictable. But I wanted an adventure.

We did ok. For a while. We were both so absorbed in our careers and happy enough, and then when Claire was born, the whole precarious house of cards came tumbling down."

I can tell Marco is listening intently. Part of me wishes he wasn't. I am not particularly proud of this period of my life.

"Jeff started resenting my career and insisted that I quit and stay at home. It was really hard for me to do that. I just became more and more indignant until it didn't work anymore to even be in the same room. It was ugly for a long time but eventually we found our way back to being good co-parents and even friends. He's happily involved now, about to start a brand new family and it's all very exciting for him."

"Did he cheat on you?"

"Jeff is not one to be neglected very long and when the trouble started began a relationship with a nurse at his hospital. What a cliché, right? The reality is that they're a perfect couple. She's very young, and completely interested in subsuming her life for his needs. I have to admit she's a lovely girl and much better suited to him than I ever was. She's great with the girls and I'm happy with their relationship."

I pause to collect myself. "What about your marriage, Marco? What happened?"

"Like you, we did ok too. We were very convivial. Like brother and sister. My father began doing business with her father when we were kids, and the families became friends. We grew up together, and I was so obsessed with following in my father's footsteps that I just made the decision I would marry this Italian girl, just as my father had. I didn't think it through, obviously, and well... we know how it ended.

The irony is that we would have probably had a lifelong friendship, if it hadn't been ruined by forcing it to be romantic."

"What exactly ended the marriage?"

I hope I'm not being too intrusive, but I am desperately curious.

"My career started taking off right after the boys were born so I left the firm I was working for and decided to start my own. I built this very successful company from nothing but the price was time away from my family. It was really painful for me and Anna was very unhappy to be alone most of the time with our two boys while I was traveling the world.

She thought it was very glamorous but the reality is that it was brutally hard work. Because all the intimacy was gone, she was convinced I was having an affair, or many affairs, I don't know. She couldn't get it out of her mind. I couldn't handle how she questioned everything I did. Every interaction we had felt like an interrogation. I couldn't do anything right, in her eyes."

"Were you?"

"Was I?" He didn't understand.

"Were you having an affair?"

"No, Monique. No, I wasn't and it wasn't because I didn't have the opportunity or even the desire. It was because I didn't want to be that person. It would have been the easiest thing in the world for me to have someone in my bed, every night if I wanted. But I didn't. I wouldn't. Anyway, she wouldn't believe me and she… she… had an affair. She says it was to spite me. I don't know. It involved someone very close to me and that was the end. I couldn't…"

I can't believe what I'm hearing.

"Did she stay with this guy?"

"Oh, no. He wasn't interested in that. He just wanted to have her and spite me."

"Wow. This doesn't sound like a very good friend, Marco."

"No, it wasn't a friend. It was actually my brother."

I know my face is frozen in shock and disbelief.

"Holy shit, Marco!! That is… too much to believe. Do you still speak?"

"Of course. We are family. And frankly, that's who he is, Monique. He… I don't want to defend him but now I know better. That's all."

I know nothing I can say will be worthy or appropriate, so I am silent.

He startles me with the first words after our quiet moment.

"That feels good."

I realize I've been gently stroking his chest and stomach.

"Your skin, Marco. It's the color of the most perfectly buttery caramel."

"I wish I was nearly as delicious as you make me sound."

I bet you are, I think.

"You take very good care of your body. It's very impressive. You must spend hours at the gym."

"Not really hours, but I do go. I like the feeling of finding my limits. And pushing them. What I really love is soccer. I try to play a few times a week with a league I'm in. They're all much younger than I am so I get quite a good workout!"

He pauses as if looking for the right words.

"Do you like my body?"

I am awed at his courage to say what I would find impossible.

"Marco, your body is… flawless. You are a very handsome man."

He tilts my face up to look in my eyes. I realize for the first time, in the bright sunlight, that our eyes are the same color. An unusual hazel hue that I rarely see. Mine is from one brown-eyed and one blue-eyed parent. Maybe his are too.

"I'm very happy you think that, Bella. You know I think you are remarkable – physically and otherwise."

"Thank you." Keeping it simple forces me to swallow all the denials I would have expressed.

I slide my face back down and kiss his chest several times before settling back into a contented quiet.

I notice the tone of our relationship shifting, becoming much softer and more intimate. We connect like adults who have acknowledged their attraction for each other. He holds me, either on the lounger or in the water, where I let myself sink into his supportive arms and set all my insecurities free. I haven't been with a man like this in so long, but Marco is making it feel easier than any man in my life ever has. The idea that this is too good to be true never strays more than a moment away from my thoughts, however.

The afternoon passes too quickly, and soon it's time for me to get ready for Nora's meeting. We've been lying on the lounger, in and out of luxurious naps. It is excruciating to pull myself out of his arms.

"I have to go now, Marco. Nora has a reception tonight, and I promised I would make an appearance."

He holds me against him. "I understand, Bella, although I would happily spend the rest of the day here with you."

I force myself to separate our bodies. "It was so nice to spend the day with you, like this, so relaxed."

"And it's only a few hours until we see each other again, right?"

Is he questioning whether I still want to see him later? His modesty keeps surprising me.

"Of course. I'm really looking forward to it."

"Me too."

I notice him gathering his belongings. "You don't have to leave on my account. Stay, and enjoy the rest of the day."

"I will walk you to your room, if you don't mind."

The chivalry is really working for me. We stroll back inside, never losing touch with each other. He pauses uncomfortably when we get to my door. He can't possibly be nervous about kissing me goodbye, can he?

"I want to ask you something."

"You are a man of many questions, Marco."

His laugh lightens the tension. "I want to invite you to the wedding. As my guest. Actually your sisters too. What do you think?"

I must have the most dumbfounded expression on my face, as if I have suddenly gone deaf and mute, which causes him to repeat the whole thing.

Still, I have to ask, "You want me to be your date for the wedding? Don't you already have a date?" What a stupid question.

"Well, I was going to go with my sister, but she had to cancel at the last minute, because two of the kids are sick. Does that mean you will come?"

"I'm just so surprised, Marco. Can you really do that?"

"Of course I can. Besides, this is Vegas. Half the casino floor will probably be crashing anyway."

I'm a bit lost for words. "I would love to go, but I have to check with the girls, of course. And Nora's award ceremony on Sunday..."

"The wedding does not start until that night, after Nora's event."

"You've thought of everything, haven't you?"

"I doubt it. But I want you to come with me. If you want to."

"I don't see why not. I'll let you know for sure tonight, after I talk to the girls. And none of us have anything to wear!" The extent of my idiocy cannot be overstated.

"You're kidding, right? I would be very happy if you wore those shorts from last night. Although I might not be such a gentleman next time around."

I catch my breath, and he notices. If this man knew how much I want him, I'm sure he would run screaming from this hotel.

"Thank you, Marco. For the invitation. It really is too kind. Like everything you've done..."

"Maybe I am pursuing pleasure as well," he says, provocatively.

"I'll see you in a few hours," I say as I open the door to my room. I turn around and kiss him lightly on the lips.

*　　　*　　　*

Nora's event passes in a daze. I try to be present, but I keep thinking about my afternoon with Marco. What will our dinner date bring? And is it too much time together? Will he grow tired of me?

Since I would be coming directly from Nora's dinner I told Marco I would meet him at dinner. He was not happy about that, finding it lacking in chivalry. He wanted to pick me up from my room but I insisted. It will save us time, I think.

When the time comes, I wish I had time to go up to the room and freshen up. This is going to be an important night, I hope.

As I approach, I see him standing at the entrance to the restaurant, wearing the most beautiful suit I think I have ever seen. He could easily be a superstar. Almost too handsome to be real.

He beams at me as I get closer. I suppose he approves of my choice for tonight, a burgundy silk crepe with a bit of flounce and a requisite display of leg. I am wearing my lucky shoes. I feel good.

"It has only been a few hours, Bella, but it feels like a new day to see you again. And again more beautiful than the last time. I believe you must be magical."

"Thank you," I say as I move toward him and offer two lingering kisses, one on each cheek. You look wonderful," I add as I gently stroke the lapels of his suit. All I can think about is taking it off him. Yes, tonight will be our night.

The restaurant is breathtaking. Sleek and modern, in just my aesthetic, while still being utterly romantic. This is an inspired choice, and nearly impossible to get a reservation, I have heard. Emile had mentioned this place, and apparently told the chef that I might be coming. He had set up an introduction, if I chose to pursue it. I'm not sure tonight is the right time to engage with the chef and do some networking. My other needs are currently taking precedence over my career.

Dinner is nearly flawless. I laugh so hard that I literally cry. The conversation stops only when a moment of silence is what we want. We talk about family and pleasure and beauty. He talks about his kids - they sound like amazing men - and I offer funny stories about my girls.

I even tell him about the reality of my career. How I am at a crossroads and had been dishonest about what I said on the plane. "I used to be a chef," I tell him apologetically. "Now, I'm back to being an apprentice."

"No my dear, I don't believe you. You are a chef. It is clear in every cell of your body. Maybe that is not what you are doing now, but it is always who you are being."

He takes my breath away. I want to say, *let's get out of this fabulous restaurant and go up to your fabulous room. There I want you to take me completely and listen when I tell you that I love you. You are too good to be true and yet here you are. With me.*

Nothing comes out of my mouth. What can I say?

"Did you talk to your sisters about the wedding?" A welcome change of subject.

"Yes, and it works out perfectly."

"Yes, Nora's ceremony ends at 5 and the wedding starts at 6. You will all come. I think Lizzy already accepted Esteban's invitation."

"Yes, my baby sister is smitten."

"They both are."

This is wonderful. I am actually dying to go the wedding, wondering what Marco will be like in a sea of eligible single women, as can be found at most weddings. This is good. Really good.

"Marco, this is so generous of you, to invite us all. Are you sure it's ok… all these extra guests at the last minute? I know what it's like to plan a wedding."

"Remember, it's Las Vegas, Bella. They expect to invite most of the hotel."

"Thank you. Now I have a purpose for the inevitable shopping trip tomorrow."

"I suppose that means no silver shorts?"

"Correct. They've had their one airing, and will now be permanently retired."

"Maybe I can negotiate a private viewing?"

Now it's my turn to change the subject. "Will you be stuck in the rehearsals all day?"

"Part of the day, yes. But I will still have plenty of time for you, don't worry." A wink and that smile again. "Then we have the rehearsal dinner but I don't think it will go very late. Is that ok?"

"Of course it's ok. You are free to do as you wish, as far as I know. And I do realize that your sole purpose for being in Las Vegas is not actually my entertainment. I'm ok with it. Really." I'm hoping he gets my humor.

"Thank you for being so considerate and understanding." His sly smile indicates he's in on the joke. "I promise to make it up to you. In whatever way you wish."

This is getting juicy. "Well there's nothing to make up, but I appreciate the offer, which I might accept anyway." Hot. Very hot. All the innuendo is tickling the middle of my body again.

Dinner is coming to an end and I need to decide. Will I reach out to the chef while I have the opportunity, or will I bypass it to stay present to the man in front of me? I am torn. And then the door opens.

Marco calls our server over and starts to transmit a message to the chef about his enjoyment of his dish. How tender the lamb was, and the perfection of the accompaniments. His eloquence and grace makes an impression on the waiter and me.

I haven't told Marco about my connection, but when the server is about to walk away with the message, I stop him. "Actually..." I say, "would you mind telling the chef that Monique Malone is here? Oh, and that I really enjoyed my meal as well. It was spectacular."

"Does Chef Turot know you?" the server asks with raised eyebrows.

"Yes, he is expecting me," I respond.

"Yes, yes I will tell him right away."

I can feel Marco staring at me.

"You are remarkable."

"Why?"

"You know the chef and you didn't say anything. What else are you hiding from me? You are really some celebrity chef, and probably have your own restaurants around the world. And a reality show, right?"

"Very funny. Marco, I'm sure you are much more famous than I will ever be. It's just that my old friend Emile, who is nearly a celebrity, wanted me to meet some people while I was here. To further my reentry back into the wild world of food. HE is the well-connected one, not me."

Marco is shaking his head at me, thinking I am being falsely modest. But I'm not. I really am a nobody.

Out comes the chef, out to prove me wrong. A jovial round man, who might have been Santa Claus in a previous life, comes barreling toward us all arms and smiles.

"Monique, Monique, I am so glad you came! What a wonderful surprise! How is Emile? That rascal still causing trouble everywhere he goes? Oh my goodness, this is so wonderful!!"

I had just assumed he was French, like Emile, but the accent is definitely Spanish. He picks me up out of my chair and gives me a great big bear hug. For a moment I think he might not let go. What a warm wonderful man, so different than the typically manic and antisocial chef.

"Emile tells me you are thinking of going back into the fire. Brave choice! I don't know that I would do it," he laughs and pats his significant belly. Definitely Santa Claus. "Anything I can do to help, I'm happy to. But I will miss your articles in the magazine. You are such a good writer. If you wrote a book, I would read it. Maybe you can still write on the side, even though I know already that is ridiculous. To be a chef takes a whole life!"

"Thank you so much, Chef. Your restaurant is beyond description. And everything was perfect. My friend Marco also sent you a message about his dish."

Marco stands up and greets the chef in Spanish. They kiss on both cheeks, in that way I find so sexy. I am quickly left behind in the trails of Spanish. They speak as if they are long lost friends, so happy to meet another Latin comrade. I can decipher only a few words of each sentence. I think they are talking about the towns they are from. Or not. My Spanish is abysmal.

Now they are looking at me and speaking. Uh oh, I don't like this, but I do hear something about beautiful woman, talented chef. They are having a Monique adoration society meeting. This is getting embarrassing. Marco takes my hand and kisses it. What the heck is going on now?

There is another flurry of words, followed by laughing and hugging. I really better get my Rosetta Stone Spanish lessons out of the closet again. Or maybe I will have my own private tutor? Hopeful again…

Marco takes my hand, and says, "Yes, I know I am a very lucky man."

"My dear, I am so glad you were able to come in. We might not have time tonight but I would love to talk to you anytime. I really mean it. The way Emile speaks of you, I know you have something special. You need to be in a major kitchen feeding the people!"

I am stunned. I don't want to overreact in front of either of these men, but I am all shrieks and celebrations on the inside. I feel like some switch has been turned on in my life, and all of a sudden amazing men and world-class chefs think I'm fabulous. It is almost too much for me to take in.

I promise to re-connect with the Chef and feel incredibly grateful to Emile. I am pleasantly surprised to hear how well Emile thought of me. And I know it wasn't because I was a great lover.

"Tell me about Emile. He is a friend of yours?"

I have to be strategic about answering. Our history is complicated.

"Emile and I met my first day in culinary school. Our new class was being shown around as he entered one of the rooms, and the head of the school stopped mid-sentence to hug and kiss him. They were both quintessentially French. Apparently, he had funded part of the newest wing, and was a regular fixture in the school. He noticed me right away, claiming I was one of the few attractive women in culinary school."

I avert my eyes, realizing the conceit in my statement.

"I have no idea about how the women look in culinary school, but you, Monique, stand out in any group."

I give him a slightly embarrassed smile and continue.

"Emile sat with our small group at mealtimes, and we fell into an easy friendship. He became my mentor, my confidante and my greatest cheerleader. I never really understood what he saw in me in those early days, but he claimed he had a nose for genius and he could smell it on me. As I finished school, and embarked on my career, our relationship changed and we became more like peers. He asked my advice on chefs, restaurants and investments. Even personal stuff. We hung out like old friends or family. People often thought we were related. Emile is one of the most important people to me, and I'm so grateful for his presence in my life."

I leave out an important part and it sits uncomfortably on the tip of my tongue.

"Was he ever more than a friend?"

The question I've been dreading. Be honest, or keep it clean?

"When Jeff and I split up, and he began his very public affair, Emile and I... well... we started sleeping together. He provided a sexual outlet for me when I needed one."

I really don't want to continue. This is too much.

"How long were you together?"

"Not very long. It was fun, at first. Our friendship made it easy to be lovers. His bright star in the food world gave us access to all the best restaurants and a social calendar to fill all my nights. Both of us knew, but never said, that this was a fleeting moment, but we took full advantage.

Then I saw him with a young waitress at a trendy cafe. I knew better than to think I was the only one for him, but the idea of my sharing myself so freely with him and him sharing himself so freely with whomever just grossed me out. He was sad when I told him we were back to being friends but he understood. That, and I'm sure he had better (and younger) fish to fry."

"There weren't any hard feelings?"

"I was sore, I guess. But I knew what I was getting into with him. It wasn't like Jeff's betrayal."

I need to swallow, but don't want to look like I'm getting emotional. Even though I am. Marco's next question gets my immediate attention.

"Are you seeing anyone right now?" He wraps his fingers around my hand and squeezes.

"No. Not at all. As single as a girl can get."

Of course I want to ask the same question, but I'm scared. I do it anyway.

"How about you? Anyone in your life?"

"No. I... haven't... I'm not seeing anyone."

Underneath the implacable look I try to keep on my face, I am grinning from ear to ear.

Marco begins to lead me out of the restaurant, and I hold my tongue from asking where we are going. We get in a taxi. Are we going back to his room? Does he have another event planned?

I feel unexplainably secure, even in my complete ignorance. I trust him and this is a very unusual feeling. Some other activity to continue our night would be nice, but I do not need or expect it. We are pretty good at entertaining each other even with nothing else.

I really can't believe how we have spent nearly the whole day together. I am no longer worried he will grow tired of me, at least not in the short term. I know he likes me, and can clearly feel his attraction.

Marco directs the driver to another hotel. We are not going back to the Wynn, which means it isn't straight back to his room. Part of me feels silly for being disappointed, but only just slightly.

I turn toward him to say something, I'm not quite sure what, but find my lips on his. It is the first time we have kissed tonight and it feels wonderful. We are getting used to each other and finding our rhythm. Marco's attentiveness reaches every interaction we have, and I can feel him trying to understand what I want. He lingers in the right places and grows stronger and more insistent as my breath quickens.

I am surprised and slightly embarrassed to find we have arrived at our destination. I just want to keep kissing this man. And more.

I sit in the cab as Marco walks around and opens my door. I feel like a woman around him – not a mother, not a middle child, not a struggling chef. It's not an issue of shying away from my power, but of embracing the delight in being treated a certain way. He kisses my hand and arm and neck as we stride across the casino, never once losing contact with me. Everything around me fades into the background. All I know is the two of us.

I can hear a beautiful singer. Exquisitely beautiful. No cheesy lounge singer. Something exemplary. Marco turns to me as we stand at the entrance of this small club and says, "I know you must have been curious about where we were going, and what we were doing. I really appreciate that you trusted me. It means a lot to me."

"I heard what you said about your wife's interrogations. I know that really hurt you. I didn't want to do the same thing."

I am relieved that I followed my instinct and kept my mouth shut. I realize it was a very lucky break on my part, given my tendency to want to know all details at every moment. Not knowing and just trusting was feeling remarkably good.

"Besides, I trust you." I did not mean for that to come out. I don't trust anybody, betrayal oftentimes the air that I breathe. What is happening to me?

I see Marco is touched but he says nothing. Instead, we follow the sound of that magical voice. I think of my mother, who had spent her youth singing and performing. Maybe she would have been in a place like this, if it had existed. I miss her so deeply.

"Where are you, my dreamer?"

"Sorry," I say sheepishly.

"No need to be sorry. Let me join you."

We sit down and I tell him about my mother. I can hardly believe how honestly I speak to him, even about things that are very personal. My typical way is to conceal and withhold. None of that is possible with Marco. It crosses my mind that maybe I no longer need all the protection that secrecy afforded me.

He reaches his arm around me and gives me a big squeeze. "I can't imagine how magnificent she must have been. Would you like to tell me more about her?"

"Our mother was the most beautiful woman I have ever seen, with this other-worldly quality. She and Dad were so happy, for so many years, and they ended up leaving this world together, which was pure romance for them, but pure tragedy for us. Mom was so full of love but there was something about her that you could tell held some sadness. As if she was missing something or someone.

We would often catch her daydreaming (probably where I got my own habit), but she would never talk about it. Instead she would make up these fantastical stories about other worlds and creatures. And she would sing. My gosh, our mother could mesmerize any human being with her voice. Her famed career all happened before we were born, but none of us question that it had been remarkable.

When it came time to raise her kids, she dropped everything and devoted herself completely to us. Danny's death nearly killed her. She could not believe her little boy was gone, even though he was a grown man and had lived a beautiful life. Then she and Dad disappeared in that boating accident, which nearly killed the rest of us."

Marco exhaled deeply. He clearly didn't know what to say.

"Enough for now. I just want to enjoy being here. With you." I lean over and kiss him. I feel my body move towards him of its own will. This taking it (relatively) slow is fine most of the time, but occasionally I feel crazed with desire. Like a fire that needs to be tended immediately.

All of me. Why not take all of me.

I begin to sing the melody, one of my very favorites, while Marco watches me with great amusement. I know I don't have the musical talent of my mother and sisters, but I can hold a tune. And it isn't an area around which I have a lot of self-consciousness so I sing freely. He smiles at me, that mesmerizing smile, and I enjoy his pleasure.

"You didn't tell me you could sing."

"That's because I can't. I am the only non-singer in my family."

"You call that not singing? Hmmmm. I am just noticing that the more I know you, the more talents I discover. Where does it end?"

"Oh, probably in about 1 minute. You've seen everything. It's all downhill from here."

"Isn't downhill a good thing?"

"I guess. I always forget which is the good one, uphill or downhill. It never really made sense to me."

We share a laugh and I snuggle into his shoulder for the next few songs. He orders an extravagant bottle of champagne, which I drink with great enjoyment. There is nothing in my life, at this moment, that isn't absolutely perfect.

I can feel myself getting tired, even sleepy, and don't want that to end our evening. I can't deny I am feeling the effects of our previous night out. Marco notices me starting to fade, and says, "Let's go."

Before I know it we are in the elevator at the Wynn, headed up to the penthouse. The decision is made with a silent look - he asks me with his eyes which button to press and I say yes to his choice. Sleepy or not, I am going to be with this man tonight. We are quickly running out of time in Vegas.

I walk straight towards the window for that amazing view. It is still mesmerizing. He steps lightly behind me, brushes my hair to the side and begins to kiss the back of my neck. This is my favorite move of all time. I let him linger there for some time, giving soft sounds of positive feedback to let him know he should continue.

"Bella, what do you want?" he whispers.

Without turning around I answer, "I want you to ask me again." I am being subtle, obtuse even. Will he understand what I am saying?

He spins me around to face him and looks straight into my eyes. I can only imagine what he can see with his penetrating gaze. My sly smile reveals that I am testing him, and his eyes demonstrate understanding.

"Will you stay with me tonight?"

He gets it. He really gets it. Part of me is expecting him to fail the test, to not understand my subtle reference.

"Yes," I say with my eyes and my lips. Then I lean towards him and offer him my mouth, which he takes willingly.

He leads me to the bedroom, which is as magnificent as the rest of the suite. They are serious about making people feel like royalty up here. I stop him before he gets to the bed and begin to kiss his face, then down his neck. I stroke his shoulders and arms as I take off his jacket. I am moving slowly, partly out of building anticipation and partly out of my own nervousness. I'm not going to blow this one.

I linger on each button of his shirt, taking my time to reveal his phenomenal body, adorned by a small patch of hair that begins in the middle of his chest and ends at the top of his pants. Dark black hair, interspersed with gray and silver, is perfectly set off by his tan skin. When his shirt falls to the ground, all I can think is how this man belongs in an underwear ad.

He tries to pull me in close and I edge him backwards, towards the bed. "Sit down," I tell him. Ordering him around is giving me a warm rush of excitement. I begin to kneel down in front of him, moving in slow motion, and I see him catch his breath. I know this looks sexy, and he must be wondering what I'm going to do down there. Did I mention this is fun?

I run my hands down his legs, filling him with anticipation, then pick up his right foot and take off his shoe. He watches me like a hawk, perhaps not believing his eyes. Off with the other shoe and for the briefest moment, I think about having him in my mouth. No, that would have to wait for another time.

I stand up halfway, kiss him intensely, then kneel astride him, one leg on either side. He can't hold himself back any more and pulls me in. My legs open around him, which lifts my dress above my hips, revealing the entirety of my lower half.

He slips his hands around my hips and pulls my buttocks in to him. I can feel him erect, pulsing for me, while he rubs our bodies together.

"Why are you still fully dressed?" he asks.

"Actually, we are probably wearing the same number of items now." This isn't even true because all I have on is my dress and my underwear - a very skimpy, very sexy silk thong. Not even a bra with my form-fitting dress.

His hands are deliciously warm on my bottom and up my back. Those amazing hands take my dress, now covering only half of my body, and peel it off the rest of me. A moment of self-conscious terror fills me. Ok, this is it. This is the moment he decides I am horrifying and leaves in disgust. The body I work pretty hard to maintain is still that of a 40-something mom. Not perfect, to say the least. Everything my swimsuit cleverly concealed is now on full display.

As if he can read my mind, he says, "You are the sexiest woman I have ever seen. I want every part of you."

I reach for his belt buckle and begin to fumble. Buttons and ties are ok, but buckles leave me clumsy and un-coordinated. Instead of taking over, he leaves me to sort it out. He really enjoys my undressing him, I realize.

I move off of him to take his pants off and there we are left with just his underwear, my skimpy thong and miles of skin. How will this proceed? I am considering what I will do next when Marco takes over.

He moves me onto my back and begins to caress my body with his hands, and explore with his mouth. His pace is just right for me, taking his time despite both of us being so aroused. He starts out very gently with my breasts, my abdomen, my legs, always leaving me wanting just a bit more. He forms a spiral of kisses starting around my navel and broadening out to cover my entire torso. Every time he approaches the top of my thong I start. It is like a small electric shock.

And there he lingers, just going back and forth, moving the silk band just millimeters down at a time. I know I'm not going to let him go all the way down, (much too intimate for this stage), but the way he is playing with me is really working.

I bring his head back up to mine, and kiss him like I mean it. His body slides on top of mine and I exhale, letting the weight of his body settle. It has been so long since I felt a man on top of me. I want to stay there for a long time. Then I think about slowly lowering his underwear, but feel a pang of uncertainty. Will we proceed right to intercourse if I do that? Will these explorations that I am enjoying so much stop? Am I having second thoughts about having sex with him?

His hands stroke the length of my body, this time moving underneath my panties. I am already so wet that his fingers slide easily between my folds. And there he begins to touch me, slowly, delicately, with complete focus.

A flash of recognition and surprise comes to me as I remember a book Lizzy had given me about the female orgasm. I had unfortunately never been successful in convincing my partners to learn the particular technique, which was an issue for me as no man had been able (or willing?) to bring me to orgasm for a very long time. Marco is doing it now, whether he knows it or not.

His lips find my mouth, my face, my neck, my breasts while he just continues to stroke without urgency or impatience. He seems completely content just to watch me and touch me.

I can feel the climbs and falls becoming stronger and stronger until fear arises instead. This is too vulnerable - here with this man I hardly know, completely exposed and about to release myself into pure pleasure - and I stop myself. I feel tension begin to replace the heat, and as quickly, so does he.

His face moves to my ear and he whispers, "I am here, Monique. Let yourself go and I will catch you. I promise."

He increases the pressure slightly, of his mouth and his fingers, until I am pushed to the top. I step off the edge of the cliff and fall deeper and deeper into the sensations. Waves of orgasm roll through my body as I wonder if time may have stopped. I want to mentally chronicle how indescribable and unexpected this is, but my body refuses to let my attention go. I can hardly look at Marco, although I know he is trying to catch my eyes. It is just short of too much for me.

When the physical sensations dampen, I roll towards him, and curl my body into his. He holds me while I fight the overwhelming urge to cry. If I could have stood up, I would have gone running out of that room. But I can't move. I feel scared and naked and certain that the higher I ascend, the more devastating the inevitable fall will be.

I can't imagine what he must be thinking, the woman in his bed having gone fetal and fighting tears. He does not say anything, but keeps his body wrapped around mine.

And then I wake up. The room is filled with light and it takes me several moments to understand where I am. The evening recreates itself until I remember why I am in this strange room, in an empty but disheveled bed. I hear soft clanging outside the door. I am not alone.

As soon as Marco enters the room, wearing low slung sweatpants and carrying two large white mugs, my humiliation blooms. He had taken care of me and instead of reciprocating, I fell asleep. Crying. Can I summon any magic to make myself disappear? What must this man think of me - selfish and weepy? Trying not to appear shell-shocked and ashamed, I look at him and smile.

"Good morning my beautiful Monique." The sound of his voice begins to melt me again. "Tea, darling? I hope that's what you wanted."

"Yes, yes, that's perfect. And so thoughtful. Thank you."

"How did you sleep?"

"I don't know. I mean... I must have passed out. I'm so sorry. I didn't even drink very much..."

"There is nothing to be sorry about." He sits next to me on the bed. "I am so happy you stayed with me. It was wonderful to be with you."

His face is full of contentment, but I can hardly stop myself from saying, was it? I know this man thinks I am a horrible person, and is plotting how he is going to drop me as soon as he can. There is no doubt in my mind.

"I have a fitting in about half an hour, but I want you to stay here as long as you want. I think you need some rest."

Aha! He is leaving! Ample evidence of his disgust with me.

"No, no, that's ok. I should be going." I try to wriggle myself out of the bed, while staying completely covered with the sheets. It is an exercise in clumsiness and awkwardness and immaturity. I don't care.

"Why do you hide yourself from me?" He is looking at me quite confused. "And I don't want you to leave right now. Please, have your tea. Stay here. I am not ready to say goodbye."

He gently moves the hand that is holding up the sheet and lets it fall. I am naked. He moves in towards me and wraps his arms around me.

"What a beautiful night I had with you. Thank you for sharing yourself with me. It was... well... I hope it was ok for you."

I can't believe what I am hearing. This man is thanking me for letting him pleasure me. I freeze, unable to make this situation make sense. This guy is either the greatest playboy ever in the history of time, or... something else too much for me to imagine. The love of my life?

"Marco, I'm so embarrassed about what happened." I don't want to talk about this and yet here I am, doing it. "I can't believe I just fell asleep. You must think I'm so rude and selfish. And I am.

I just don't know what to say. And how emotional I got. You must think I'm a complete lunatic."

"Aaah. I understand. That is why you want to cover yourself, and leave quickly?"

I nod.

He looks away as he moves his head almost imperceptibly up and down. "It does not happen very often in my life that I connect with someone like this. I did not come to Vegas to hook up. Quite the opposite in fact." (What did that mean?) "Monique you are unlike any woman I've ever known and I certainly don't think you are any of those things you said.

I don't really know what happened for you last night, although I would love for you to tell me, if you want. What I know is that I was so happy that you stayed with me, and that you opened yourself to me, and that I was able to be a part of something that was enjoyable for you. It was wonderful for me and I don't feel like I missed anything."

I am going to cry again. *NO Monique, keep it together*, I scream in my own head. *You do not need to keep falling apart in front of this guy. He is not the recipient of all your pain. He showed up in your life, has been awesome so far, and may or may not betray you like the others. You do not need to expose yourself any more.*

"It was... unexpected... for me. I haven't had so many good experiences lately and it brought some things up. It was really nice for me, no doubt, and I don't want you to think otherwise. You have been absolutely wonderful." Clearly I have lost any control over what's coming out of my mouth. It's as if I drank a truth serum or something.

"Thank you for being honest with me. And trusting me too." He slips under the covers, brings me to him and begins to kiss me softly at first, then passionately. Our bodies intertwine and everything from last night rises in me again. This man can have anything, anyone he wants, and just keeps choosing me. I don't get it.

I want to explore his body, magnificent as it is, to take my time, and feel him and taste him. I want to show him that I can give as well as receive, that I am intensely attracted to him. But he just wants to give to me. He takes charge in that beautiful bed, and the small part of me that wants to resist, to be in charge, is consumed by all the pleasure I am experiencing. He takes the covers off of me and looks at my fully naked body. He refuses to let me avert my eyes. He implores, *Look at me. I want you to see me looking at you.*

The time passes too quickly and he is going to be late for his appointment. We leave the suite in a flurry, promising to keep in touch during the day. He has lots of wedding events, including the rehearsal dinner, and I will be with my sisters, shopping for dresses then taking Nora out for a family dinner.

"Will I see you tonight?" he asks.

"You mean you haven't had enough of me yet?"

"Actually, I haven't had nearly enough of you."

The way he says that nearly buckles my knees.

"We will have an early night tonight - the bride's orders - so I will be here. In the room. When you get back from dinner."

His hinting is much more charming than subtle. He is often so direct and commanding but can also be this bashful boy. It dissolves my heart every time.

I don't want to answer directly. Some ridiculous vestige of playing hard to get, so I say, "I will let you know what we decide to do."

"I'll be waiting for you."

He walks me down to my room, even though I tell him he doesn't have to. Chivalry is not optional, he declares.

I open my door to find Lizzy going through my clothes.

"Hey Nik! I need to borrow your white t-shirt. Mine is dirty."

"Hey Lizzy. Thanks for asking."

"Hey Marco! Where are my kisses?" We laugh as he enters the room and gives Lizzy her two kisses. What a good man he is...

"Oh, you've decided to grace us with your presence." The voice from the other room is unmistakable. "Shall I assume you've not come back a virgin?" Nora opens the door and has a start when she realizes that Marco is also in the room. I shake my head in disgust at her, but do not speak.

"Good morning Marco," she says in a tone that is sheepish and defiant at the same time.

"Nora." He kisses her on both cheeks. Lizzy stands frozen, unable to speak, perhaps waiting for Nora to apologize for her rude remark. I know better than to expect an apology coming from our sister.

"Have a beautiful day ladies," he says as he strides towards the door, holding my hand. "And don't worry Nora, I have returned her as intact as she came to me. For now."

He kisses me at the door, hands me his key and says, "Use it."

I feel as if we've condensed 6 months of relationship into 2 days and I've just been asked to move in together. For a moment I forget my sister's awful behavior and giggle like a little girl.

"See you later," is all I can manage.

As soon as the door closes, I turn to glare at Nora. Sometimes she just goes too far.

"He told **you**!!" Lizzy scoffs at Nora.

"I didn't know he was in here!!! No need to make such a big deal about it. The real question is how come you're still 'intact'. Is he a monk or something?"

"No he's not a monk, not that that's any business of yours anyway. God, Nora, is it really that hard to not be offensive every minute of your life??"

"That was harsh, Nik," says Lizzy.

"I deserved it," Nora says, which leaves us both open-mouthed and stunned. "Let's start over, ok? I'm so glad we're spending the day together. And Nik, I really want to hear about your night. You two are looking like the king and queen of Vegas. Is there going to be a double wedding tomorrow?"

"Shut up," I say with a girlish grin. "Let me get ready so we can get this day started, ok?"

"OK," they say in unison as they sit down on the bed and watch me expectantly.

"Boy I'm really glad we paid for 3 rooms here," I say sarcastically.

"I'm sorry, WHO paid for three rooms??" asks Nora, who is bankrolling this particular jaunt.

"Fine." I resign myself to an audience while I get ready. An audience that plies me with questions faster than I can answer them. Why didn't we have sex? What did we do, exactly? What did we talk about? Did I meet the chef? Am I going to sleep with Marco tonight?

I answer what I can, and don't withhold much. I downplay my crying stint, although they can probably tell I am doing that. My sisters are well aware of both my emotional nature and my sordid history with heartbreak.

We are in disbelief that not even 48 hours has passed. I know this is a recurrent pattern for me – falling hard and fast. Lizzy too, although the inevitable crash always leaves her a bit less scarred than I have been. Even Nora and Sam wasted no time. I wonder what it is about us that makes us so vulnerable? Able to fall in love so quickly. These two days have been a surprise for me, certainly, but the pace feels natural. Perhaps we're each trying to find our version of our parents' love-at-first-sight magical story.

The three of us skip out of the room, credit cards ready for some major damage. There's no shortage of shopping opportunities, and we plan to take advantage of most of them. Dresses are top on the list, but shoes, handbags, even lipsticks fill much of the afternoon. We giggle most of the day away, giddy with the experience of being together, and our respective recent excitements. Amazing men and a prestigious award keep us in broad smiles.

I can tell from Nora's face the few times that Sam's name comes up that she misses him. She would never admit it, of course, but she wants him here, with her. Nora has such an obsession with independence that she keeps the people she loves the most at arms-distance. It gratifies her ego but I know her heart suffers. I hatch a plan as I watch her pretend she doesn't miss him as much as I know she does.

I make an excuse to back-track to a shoe store we had seen earlier, while they are still trying on dresses. As soon as I am free, I dial my phone.

"Hi Sam, it's me. Listen, I need you to do something."

7

A GUIDE AND A PLAN

The teacher Lalune was looking for found her. Actually, they found each other. Lalune accidentally barged into a meeting of the high elders, being held in her father's chambers, and heard Avanora speak.

Lalune had always been fearful of and mesmerized by the old mermaid, who spoke with such reverence about their ancient customs that it made Lalune want to know more. Lalune overheard Avanora describing the magic that only the oldest of the mermaids still had, and all the traditions that had become uninteresting to the new generation. The young ones seemed only to be concerned with treasure and fun, she said.

Avanora, whose eyes reflected something Lalune had never seen in the ocean, looked directly at Lalune when she asked the question, "What can we do to bring the passion back to our youth, instead of placating them with these all-too-easy lives?"

"You can let them pursue what they love and be who they want to be." It tumbled out of Lalune's mouth before she knew what she was doing. The council, including her father, rose in an uproar at her discourteous addition to the conversation, and she was hastily escorted out of the room.

"Who was that young mermaid?" asked Avanora.

Embarrassed and angry, Lalune's father admitted, "My daughter. Who should know better. I do apologize..."

"No need to apologize. She spoke bravely and wisely. These are the qualities I speak about. So rarely seen in our community of youth anymore."

Avanora made a point to discover where she might find the young mermaid, and came across Lalune daydreaming near the surface.

"It is not safe for you here. The land-walkers often bring their boats to this area, and go diving."

Lalune was so shocked to have been found, that she could not speak for a moment.

"How did you find me?"

"You have not kept your hiding places secret." Avanora was smiling, with a disconcerting familiarity.

"I did not realize... I just love the light up here. The constant darkness below makes me... sad."

"I see that, child. Your sadness has also evaded secrecy."

"I am sorry for barging in on your meeting. Are you here to scold me? I'm sure my father is preparing my punishment as well."

"I have no intention of scolding you. Or punishing you. I am here to help you."

"Help me? With what?" Lalune had to watch herself. These old mermaids had stronger magic. Maybe she was able to read her mind.

"Your heart's desire."

"I do not know what you are talking about." Lalune could hardly hide the fear and excitement in her voice. Could this really be the mermaid who would help her? She had to be careful. Maybe this mermaid was a spy sent by her father.

"I see." Avanora's pause lasted an eternity. "Well, my dear, you can find me at the blue cave whenever you are ready. Be well, child."

Avanora swam away, with Lalune's eyes wide, following every move. There was no time to process what had happened as Lalune's sisters swam by with their friends.

"What are you doing here?" they asked her, accusingly.

"I could ask you the same thing."

"Are you in one of your moods again?"

"No, Adina. I am not in any mood. Just minding my own business."

"You should not be up here. It is too close to the surface."

"Then why are you here?"

"We are headed toward the island, if you must know. Not hanging around, waiting to get caught. You are one fishing net away from being gone forever."

"That is an awful thing to say, Adina!" At least her younger sister was more compassionate.

"I am not planning on getting caught in any fishing lines. Thank you for your concern."

"We should go. Before the seals make a mess of things." Adina felt bad for how awful she had been to her sister lately, but she just could not understand what was wrong with her.

"Bye Lalune," they all said.

"Bye..."

*   *   *

It took days before Lalune mustered the courage to go to the blue cave. She realized that even if it was a trap, it was her only option at this point. More punishment could not be any worse than the imprisonment she was already experiencing.

"I am so glad you have decided to come see me, Lalune."

"I do not really know why I am here."

"I think you do. But we do not have to talk about that just yet. Shall we go for a swim? I would like to show you one of my favorite places."

They headed off in a direction Lalune did not recognize, away from the small island and most of the mermaids' activities.

They arrived at an outcropping of shimmering rocks that reached all the way to the surface of the water.

"It is beautiful here. I can feel... something."

"You have not lost your sensitivity. That is good. This is a special place, where our kind have come for millennia."

"What happens here?"

Avanora told her the story of a mermaid who had lived her life never feeling like she belonged in the ocean. She studied the land-walkers so closely that she eventually fell in love with one and decided to cross over.

"She did what??" Lalune could not believe her ears.

"She decided to leave us, child, and join the other world."

"What happened to her?"

"She lived and died many years ago, after a full and beautiful life as a land-walker. I knew her quite well. And although I miss her terribly, I know she had to leave us. This was not her true home."

"I do not understand..."

"Lalune, there are few creatures as blessed as we are. Our ocean kingdom is bountiful and beautiful, and brings most of us the greatest joy. But there are some, who are born... different. They do not belong here. What the Great Mother has given them belongs in the other world. If they do not heed this call, it will consume and destroy them."

"You are scaring me, Avanora."

"You are afraid because you know this is your journey. It happens rarely, but only to those who have the strength to survive the transformation, and to survive out there, where things are very different."

"I want to go back, Avanora. Please take me back."

"Of course, child. But first, I want you to feel where you are right now. The magic is strongest here, and a bit further toward shore as well. You can feel it, can you not?"

Lalune was too shaken to answer. The old mermaid relented.

"Follow me."

Lalune found it difficult to follow the old mermaid, so absorbed in the swirl of her thoughts. When they had returned to the cove, Lalune was still unable to formulate a coherent response to what she had experienced.

"Do not worry, Lalune. This is much to process right now. I know you have been holding this in for a long time, and you need time to understand. You know where to find me. I can help you."

For days, Lalune swam past the old mermaid's cove, then turned back before being seen. The fear was too much.

Then Avanora appeared at her home, again, for another council meeting. Before leaving, Avanora found Lalune, and said only these words: "The world will be changed by your voice. Let it be heard."

No one had ever spoken to Lalune so directly before, as if the sound had come from inside her own heart. It felt like a current she could not fight, and it shook the unrelenting despair from her soul and turned it into hope. She could not hide any longer, or let the fear stop her.

The two mermaids began to meet every morning. Avanora shared all she knew about making the transition, and they worked together to get Lalune ready for the biggest event of her life.

Time, fluid as it was in the underwater world, began to move much more quickly for Lalune as she immersed herself in her preparations and lessons. There were materials to collect, rituals to learn, and spells to practice so that she could walk, talk and think as the land-walkers do.

The most difficult incantation would reorganize her skeleton so she could stand and walk, but Avanora assured her that she would be fast asleep and feel no pain. There were the communication spells, so that their language would make sense in her ears, and her mouth would form the correct sounds.

Finally, there was the issue of covering her new body. The land-walkers were almost never bare, as she had been her whole life, and she had to be prepared with material to conceal herself. The details revealed themselves with each passing day.

"This is how it is done," Avanora said, weeks into their lessons. "You must arrive at the smaller rock patch, a few leagues past the area I took you, undetected, and bring your whole body out of the water. Leave plenty of time so that the full moon does not catch you too soon.

With the shell placed on your tongue, lie as still as you can until the sun rises. Repeat the spell, only to yourself, but do not let even a whisper pass your lips or the energy will not be sufficient for the transformation. Do you understand, Lalune?"

"Yes."

"Good. You are learning quickly. There are very few I would trust with this information. It could be dangerous for all of us."

"I understand." Lalune wanted to leave. Be done with the work of the day and be alone.

"I understand why your heart brings you to this crossroad. And why you want to run away from it."

"I must go now, Avanora." Lalune did not want to be sharp or impatient with Avanora, she had done so much for her, risked everything to teach her the secret. But she needed to see the place with her own eyes. Where she would leave this world behind.

She traveled slowly toward the magical spot, to see for herself how it would feel, when the time was right. Upon arriving at the larger outcropping of rocks, still a distance from her ultimate destination, Lalune felt unable to continue. She decided she was not yet strong enough, and would double her efforts in completing her studies.

She knew this was exactly what she had to do, yet grieved all she was giving up. She could not dare ask, "What if it was not worth it?"

There would be no one to take care of her, Lalune realized, which meant she had to master the intricacies of survival as a land-walker. They lived highly individual and transactional lives, compared to the mermaids, so she would have to be very clever. The sea would no longer offer her everything she needed, nor protect her from harm.

The first few days would be the most difficult, Avanora warned her. This was when her adaptation skills would be weakest, and the land-walkers would be most suspicious. The exact steps for interaction and assimilation had to be executed perfectly. There was no room for error. Or even for enjoying her new state as a land-walker until she had found safe shelter, and stayed out of the water for one entire sun cycle.

Occasionally, Lalune wondered how it was that Avanora knew so much about life on land, but those questions never had time to root with the enormity of information that filled her mind.

Avanora spoke freely about Lalune's dream of singing, and for the first time in her life, Lalune felt sure that it would happen. Only in the quietest moments, when the flurry of activity stilled, did the vast array of doubts float to the surface of Lalune's thoughts.

"What will everyone think of me for leaving our paradise?"

"You must let those thoughts go. They are fear speaking. You know what your life is supposed to be. No one's dissent can change that."

The surprises came fast and frequent in the discovery of an entirely new way of being. Lalune dedicated herself to this process like nothing she had ever attempted before, being very careful not to attract unwanted attention for her secretive life.

Lalune did not think there could be anything more that she did not know when Avanora halted their lessons one day to speak about love.

"Today, we are going to learn about your life as a woman, a female land-walker. You must know about love, dear one. It will feature prominently in your future."

"I do not care about love, Avanora. I just want to sing."

"These desires are not so different, my dear. It is important you understand what will happen to you. You will have a woman's body, but you will always have a mermaid's heart. We are unlike them, on the inside. Our feelings are more intense. You will have to be careful to see things clearly." Avanora felt from the look on Lalune's face that she had to repeat herself.

"Always remember you will never be exactly like them. We cannot remove or transform the inner spirit. It will make you softer than them, so please, be careful.

Even as a land-walker you will retain your mystical beauty, so the males will be very drawn to you. You must be cautious and use your intuition. When you find the right one, it will feel as if you have come back to the sea. Your body will feel more alive and the human world will look as beautiful as our undersea world. You must wait until that happens."

"What do you mean, the right one?"

"We love freely here, but on land it is done differently. The land-walkers search for the one true love. Many do not find each other, but you will. All your feelings will be directed towards only one man."

"Really, Avanora. I am not interested in the land-walker males. They are odd and... scary."

"Yes, I understand, my dear. But when you change, your feelings will change."

Lalune was almost embarrassed to ask this. "Will I mate with this male?"

"Yes, with one you love. It will bring you enormous amounts of pleasure. Do not fear it. You will marry and start a family, a beautiful family. They will be land-walkers and never need to know your past. Unless you tell them."

A flash of darkness crossed Avanora's face, which Lalune noticed.

"What is it? What if they come out with tails?" Lalune was honestly worried.

"They will not, but they will surely carry some of our magic, which will be wonderful for them, if they use it well. Sometimes... the offspring will need to adapt... differently. It is not something you should worry about now."

Avanora did not want to continue on this subject.

"You and your family will lead blessed lives, Lalune, if they open their hearts. The children will love in the same way we love, but their guidance might be muddied by their land-walker bodies. They may falter in a way that will not happen for you, but they will find their way. As you will find yours. Do not be afraid."

"But I am afraid."

"I know. That is how you know this is important."

"Maybe I will not be able to do it, Avanora. Maybe it will be too hard of a life for me, so used to the simplicity of our kingdom."

"I know why you say that. Your soul has not chosen the easy path, Lalune. But your calling to live a different way indicates

your ability to succeed. The seed of your new life is embedded in your visions and fantasies of it. Trust that what you have been feeling your whole life holds the truth. It is the fear that is an illusion."

"What if I cannot do it? Will I ever be able to return?"

"That is much more complicated, dear. I would not make the transformation if you are not sure. Returning is not easy."

"Please tell me. What would happen?"

"If you return, it is irreversible. You only get one chance. You would be gone from the world of land, and the ones who love you would be very sad."

"Could I bring them with me?"

"Only the one true love would be able to come with you."

"Would he become one of us?"

"Yes. He would fully transform. But this would also be irreversible. Please understand that."

"Yes, Avanora. I do," Lalune said, not quite sure if she did.

It was overwhelming, but the certainty of her decision filled her as soon as she remembered the dreams she had been carrying her whole life. There was no way to guarantee that any of it would work, from the transformation, to the life she would build as a land-walker. The only guarantee was the impossibility of her continuing life as a mermaid.

"I will do my best, Avanora. I know what I have to do. I will make my way in that world, I will be a great singer. Love or not. I must go now. See you tomorrow."

Over the next few days, Lalune could tell that something was bothering Avanora, but neither of them spoke of it. Lalune worried that perhaps Avanora disapproved of her progress.

"We have spoken of many things, my dear. You have been a good student," Avanora said.

Lalune was relieved.

"There is one last piece, however, which I must tell you. I do not want this to frighten you."

Lalune's heart gripped. Had there not been enough to take in, she thought?

"I want to know, Avanora. I must know. Whatever it is."

"You will be given something greater than any other mermaid." Avanora paused, trying to find the right words. "Changing worlds is a grand act. One which does not come without a price. In your life as a land-walker, you will have to return the gift."

"Return the gift? I do not understand."

"Something... someone very dear to you will be taken away. One life for another. Loss is a normal part of the other world. But you may feel it much more deeply than your new kind. You will experience something painful. We never know when or how. But it is inevitable."

All the possibilities flashed before Lalune. Would she lose a child, or her true love, or someone else in her life?

"You are very strong, Lalune. That is why you were chosen. You will recover."

Lalune did not know what she should be thinking, or asking.

"I do not want you to worry about this. It is woven into the material of a land-walker life. I... I did not want you to be unprepared."

"Oh, Avanora. I cannot think about this. I want to have a life in the land-walker world. I am afraid of the pain, of the difficulties. But I cannot let it stop me."

"Exactly, my child. I knew you would understand."

Lalune did not know whether she did or did not. Regardless, the plan would go forward.

"The other issue is much smaller."

Lalune was surprised that there was more. Was this not enough of a price?

Avanora continued. "Your offspring will carry something from this world."

"Yes, I know, Avanora. You told me that. But you said they would not have tails."

"Yes, that is true. Physically, they will be like all the other land-walkers."

"Then, what is it?" Lalune's voice shook.

"You will have an easy time knowing what is in your heart when it comes to love. Your senses will still be as sharp as they are here. But the children... they may falter."

"Yes, I remember you saying that as well."

"They may make poor choices. This is also normal. And carries consequences, just like it does for any creatures, on sea or land."

"Then what is the issue?"

"Should they make poor choices in love, it will be much more difficult for them. They will feel the pain more intensely, and the Great Mother will often take drastic measures to reassure balance is restored."

"This does not sound so bad, Avanora." Lalune was not sure if she had understood completely.

"No, it is not so bad. But their lives may not be free of painful situations."

Lalune felt tired by all of this information. She found it hard to not allow defeat into her heart.

"No lives are free of pain, Avanora. Is that not true?"

"Aaaah, yes, you are correct." Avanora smiled at Lalune's wisdom. "Teach them to choose wisely, Lalune. Then, it will be easier for all of you."

"I must go now, Avanora. There is too much for me to think about. I will return tomorrow, ready to begin again."

"As you wish, dearest one."

Avanora watched Lalune swim away, with a heart full of excitement and sadness.

8

UNIONS AND REUNIONS

The nearly perfect day of shopping is topped off by a surprisingly quiet dinner. Cruising around Las Vegas searching for the perfect gown has tired us out enough to dissolve any snarky attitudes. Nora picks from the list of restaurants to which I was given a special invitation, and we get the royal treatment. The magnificent meal, and my loving sisters, form a delicious experience.

We are giddy with excitement about the next day's events, and ecstatic over the food. Our connection creates a smile that circles the table throughout the entire meal. Even though I often find them ridiculous, and impossible, I adore my sisters. They teach me dedication, commitment and joy.

I don't worry about Nora – she has created a near-perfect life for herself, which includes her true love. The possibility that Lizzy just might have found the man of her dreams this weekend gives me the chills. I know that it makes no rational sense, but I can't deny that's what I see. She is one of the most loving people I have ever met, just like Dad and Danny, and deserves nothing less than to be swept off her feet by a true prince charming.

My fate is still in question. Do I dare let myself acknowledge what's been happening with Marco? I know he isn't perfect, but he appears to be as perfect for me as any human being I have known. All evidence points to 'too good to be true' but I want to believe that there is no cruel twist waiting for me. *It's so fast*, I keep telling myself. *Slow down.*

My inability to trust a man, and to trust my feelings, will have to shift if I want to create something with Marco. So far, I am the only obstacle in this potential relationship.

I leave my sisters after dinner, none of us able to put into words all we are feeling. The walk to the penthouse elevator stretches to fill a surprising amount of time. I must be walking slowly, I think to myself, although I'm vibrating with anticipation and nervousness.

As I stand outside his door with the key inches away from the lock, I breathe deeply to gather my strength. I am crystal clear on my intention for this evening: to demonstrate to this man the woman that I want to be - sexy, confident, generous and loving. The kind of woman this man deserves. I desperately want to be her.

My key slides easily in and out, and the unmistakable click lets me know it's time to enter.

I walk past my favorite view of the Vegas skyline to his bedroom, where I find Marco sitting up in bed with his reading glasses on, and a book in his lap. I watch his surprised expression change to glee as I saunter towards him.

"You made it," he says smiling so broadly I think his face might split.

"I missed you," I say as I sit down next to him, remove his glasses and relocate the book. I am determined to be courageous. And I did miss him.

In between the kisses I lightly plant on his face, he asks, "You did? How much?"

"You're about to find out," I reply.

For the next hour my mouth makes it to nearly every inch of his body, moving with infinite patience, and saving the best for last. I should have predicted that he would have a beautiful cock, but it still surprises me as I remove his pajama bottoms. Straight and hard, with skin so soft I want to rub it against my face. I've been thinking about having him in my mouth almost since we met. My oral fixation, more often satisfied by the creations of my kitchen, is undeniable.

I lick him like a lollipop, slowly and firmly, as he grows more and more excited. He gasps as my warm mouth finally surrounds him. Stroking him with my hand, I bring him in and out of my mouth, passing my wet lips then filling to the back of my throat, over and over.

He is generous with the guidance I need to get it just right – a word here, a gentle movement there, helps me know what's working. I enjoy him like the dessert after my delicious meal, and want him to feel as loved by me as I have by him when we were together previously. I invite any thoughts of self-consciousness and inadequacy to float away. Watching him experiencing so much pleasure is filling my own body with the same.

Increasing the pace, I sense his climax approaching, while his arms gently push against my shoulders, trying to move me away. I catch his eye and smile, letting him know it's ok to keep going. This is nearly the best part for me.

His groans become more insistent as he holds my shoulders strongly. I know he is on the verge of orgasm as I tease him with my tongue on the tip of his cock, then take him into my mouth again. He can't hold himself back anymore.

"Bella, I'm coming," he says breathlessly. His head arches back and his groans fill the room. The pulsing of his cock undulates through his whole body, and then mine. I hold him until my mouth is full of him.

I don't move until he has completely finished, lying quietly with his eyes closed. He looks a bit stunned, so I move slowly off of him and slide up until we are face to face. Without opening his eyes, he takes my mouth to his and kisses me deeply. His hands slide under my slip of a dress and slip it off in one move. We flip over and he is on top of me.

We pause there for a moment, contemplating the implications of what might be the next step. There isn't a single article of clothing between us. Am I ready for us to consummate our relationship? Is he, especially since he just had an orgasm?

I don't doubt his desire for me in this moment, but I can sense resistance, and am not sure if it's coming from him or me. I'm scared, even after the intimate moment we just shared. I do much better when the attention isn't on me.

We gaze at each other while our bodies find their way. The gentle rise and fall, with a tender urgency, accompanies the communication between our eyes. I want to say something but don't know what. I want him to make the decision for the both of us.

He moves my legs open with his thigh as he kisses my neck. "That was amazing, Monique. You are a woman of so many surprises."

"Glad you liked it," I say cheekily.

"I'm so happy you came here tonight. I was worried you'd had enough of me," he said, recalling what I'd said to him earlier. Our bodies are grinding. The smallest move and he would be inside me.

If only he knew how much I wanted him. How I've spent the whole day thinking about him, imagining what this night would be like, and fantasizing about our lives together. I am infatuated.

But I don't want to get hurt, and even though it's only been a few days, I am already too invested in the relationship. Will it end in heartbreak, as all the others had?

"Why would you think that I've had enough of you?"

"Everything has been so perfect. It's easy to think that it's too good to be true. And you... well, I feel you pulling away sometimes. I don't really know what that means." He lays the truth before me. Will I honor it?

"I see... You're probably right."

I'm not sure, from the look on his face whether he is surprised or relieved. "What are you afraid of, Monique?"

A ball of defensiveness rises to the back of my throat and forces the words out.

"What makes you think I'm afraid?"

"I can feel it. In your body. Maybe I'm wrong."

"Well... it's... I... just want to make sure that I'm doing the right thing."

"Do you know what the right thing is?"

"I don't know. I feel confused with you. I mean I think I do, but I'm not sure."

"What if I told you that I am afraid? I feel disoriented and... we could easily just sleep together but it feels like something more important is happening."

His clarity and honesty prevents me from continuing the charade any longer.

"I *am* afraid, Marco. You're right. I'm trying to appear much more together than I am. Inside it's a whirlwind and I can't find my legs underneath me. I'm trying so hard to make a rational decision and it's impossible. I don't understand why."

"I think it's ok, Monique, that we feel this way. I think it's exactly as it's supposed to be. We can decide to slow down and see if the fear works its way out, or just move forward. We're in charge of this situation. Do you agree?"

"Yes I do, Marco. It's just that my body is feeling such desire for you. It's my heart that... is feeling vulnerable and my mind is spinning with all the reasons this can't actually be happening."

"But it is happening. I'm right here, with you. I'm not in your imagination. I'm right here next to you. Feel me. Let's be in this together."

His gaze turns directly to me as he softly asks, "Will you tell me what you want?" I remember that same question in front of the window, our first full night together. Last night. It feels like it was months ago.

"I want to be happy," comes from my lips, which I regret almost immediately. *What a banal thing to say*, I think, especially in this moment.

"What will make you happy?"

The heart of the issue reveals itself. "Maybe I don't know."

Everything is getting too raw, then the perfect diversion pops into my head. "What do *you* want?" Turning the question around might give me time to get myself together.

"I want you to be happy." That's tricky, really tricky.

"That's not fair," I say, unable to stop myself from smiling.

"These past few days, with you, have been remarkable. Really. I don't know if I've ever experienced anything like this, connecting with someone so quickly and on so many levels. I am very attracted to you, Monique, as I hope you have seen. I don't want to presume anything. Although our current state..."

Of course. We are naked, together, in his bed. I feel foolish. And childish. And overdramatic. I'm making a mess of this otherwise perfect situation. I want to vanish.

"Does what I said upset you?"

"No," I lie.

"I don't want to upset you, Bella. I want you to feel comfortable with what happens here. And I see you are not comfortable."

Snap into shape Monique! Put on your grown-up panties, and be a reasonable adult. Right now.

"I'm not upset," lying again. "It's hard for me to tell what's really going on. It does feel too good to be true, for me too."

He moves his body completely off mine, so he can wrap his arms around me. I feel the heat of the previous moment begin to fade. He looks tired. I am frustrated by my own ineptitude.

"Do you think I am not who you think I am, or this is not what you think it is?"

"It's always so hard to tell, don't you think? Or maybe it's me. Always over-analyzing and over-complicating everything. Not wanting to trust when something feels too good. I don't want it to be this way. And yet, it's what I do. I'm sorry I'm being like this. I'm sure you just want to have a good time and I'm being so fucking dramatic about everything."

He nods, but doesn't speak. I am getting very self-conscious about being naked. I want to hide.

"I don't know if you are being fucking dramatic or not, but there's nothing here that is not as I would want it to be." His voice is very serious. "We both have pasts, Bella. We're old enough to not have escaped unharmed from love's little adventures. I'm not just looking to have fun. It would be much easier, sure. Also meaningless."

He lifts my face to see his. "We get to choose what we want Monique. You and I. Maybe there are other people or circumstances outside this room, but right here and right now it's just you and me in this bed with absolute free will."

I feel as if I'm being schooled. It's uncomfortable and slightly humiliating. Why is this such a big deal for me? I've had casual sex in my life, and yet this is so intense. I can't tell if it's a sign of danger, or a sign of importance. I am trying so hard to be logical, to get my head clear. It's as if I'm swirling underwater and can't find the surface. What is happening to me?

"I know that," I mumble.

"So let's choose." He kisses me. I kiss him back. I close my eyes and realize how nice it is to be in bed, with this man, making each other feel good. If I can let myself be in the amazing moment I'm currently living, none of the drama will be necessary.

His hand gently strokes my belly, grasps my hipbone, then slips between my legs. The fire is lit, once again.

We spend the few remaining hours of the night exploring and enjoying each other with our hands and our mouths, without crossing any lines, or triggering any more drama on my part. He studies me, and my reactions, just as he had mentioned at the pool, and I do the same for him. I ply him with questions about his likes and dislikes. The connection between us deepens even though the relationship remains unconsummated. I feel joyful satisfaction as I fall asleep in his arms. The anxiety takes a brief hiatus.

We awake in a tangle of bodies and sheets. It takes me some time to figure out where my limbs end and his begin. When I inch toward his body, he instinctively pulls me in even closer. I can feel his *good morning* to me, pressing against my leg. Our mouths meet and the heat builds very quickly. I pull him on top of me and open my legs. He slides between them and I know this is it.

I am completely ready for him, after a night of arousal and pleasure, almost not awake enough for the neurosis to begin. I feel a thrilling urgency from him.

"Please get a condom," I whisper. He moves swiftly to the side of the bed, and easily back into position. He pauses to look at me, asking me with his eyes if this is what I want.

"Yes," I say out loud, and move his hips over mine.

The initial sensation of him entering me is transcendent. This is my favorite moment of lovemaking, anticipation and recognition meeting in a delicious flash. I can hardly contain myself as he slowly fills more and more of me. He is very excited, maybe overly so, and both of us move in slow motion. I close my eyes and float in the sheer pleasure of him on top of me, inside me, breathing on my neck, kissing my face, moving with me.

He stops for a moment when my body takes him in completely, and we both catch our breath. My resistance, my uncertainty and my denial dissolve. I just want this man to continue lighting my body on fire.

He slides his palm underneath my lower back, changing the angle of my hips and enters me even more deeply. The animal-like groan from my lips is hardly recognizable to me.

"Does that feel good?"

I cannot speak. Only moan. I dance with him, surrendering to his lead, and allowing myself to be free of anything other than what I am experiencing in the moment. The truth is clear - I am loving this man and he is loving me back. I let myself fall completely into his strong arms and the power of his body. He knows the way.

It is so hard to keep my eyes open, immersed in the remarkable sensation of his rhythmic stroking, but I force myself to look at him. The pleasure in his eyes is undeniable.

Despite the fact that it has been a very long time since I had an orgasm from intercourse, I'm currently feeling the possibility. Without a doubt. Will this man break my frigid spell? Will I be able to relax enough, to not get tense and try to force things along, to let my body do what it supposedly knows how to do?

Marco has already shown me patience and skill, taking me there with his hands, but I'm not sure if I can break my own pattern.

My body wants to release into him so badly, but I feel the fear growing. I keep saying to myself, *let go, let go*, and I suppose it comes out in actual words.

"I have you. Nothing to hold onto, Bella. Let yourself go. With me."

I feel his words from a place beyond hearing. Is it possible he understands the jumbled mess that is happening inside me? He keeps proving to me over and over that that is true.

Marco moves my right leg toward my chest, opening me up even further, and begins to speed up. I can tell he is moving closer to climax, and I open my eyes to watch him. For the next several minutes we are connected in every way. I watch him growing more excited and my own body responds. As he begins to slow down, I draw him in deeper and say, "Don't stop. Please."

He resists, so I wrap my legs tightly around him, bring his face to mine and say, "Yes."

I want to feel him come inside me. I stop worrying about my own orgasm and focus on his.

He struggles, wanting to wait for me. I keep pressing him, intent on bringing him to orgasm. The conflict creates even more heat between us, and I pull his mouth to mine. And then everything slows down.

"Mi amor," he groans. Loudly. Something electric fills me as I feel him climax. The heat ignites the deepest part of my body, transforming me into something other than flesh. There is no question that I am in the right place with the right person and that I no longer need to explain what is happening between us.

Some primordial part of me knows that he is the one. It's nothing short of magical.

I don't orgasm; I wake up to a new world. The room fills with the first light of day and everything begins to shimmer. I don't breathe or need to breathe.

He continues to pulse and shake for some time, whispering, "Mi amor, mi amor."

"Si, si. Muy bien."

He laughs at my childish Spanish and the spell is broken. We are back to being a man and a woman in a bed in Las Vegas. But it's different. All my fretting is gone. I feel wonderful and beautiful and loved. No doubts can live in the bright light of this morning.

"Buenos dias, Marco."

"Buenos dias, Bella. Mi amor." I close my eyes and let him hold me as we slip into sleep again.

I wake up with my back to him, his arms wrapped around me, like tangled spoons. He is stroking my face, my breasts, my belly, and then below. He finds me wet and ready and exhales deeply. "Monique..."

He strokes me, just like the first night and I know what will happen next. Or am I dreaming? No, the electricity in my body tells me I am very much awake.

I move his hand slightly and roll onto my belly. He understands, bringing my hips back to his, and entering me from behind. His hand reaches around and begins to stroke me again. This combination, his fingers and his cock caressing me at the same time, is going to take me completely over the edge, my thoughts of frigidity a distant memory. "Marco," I think and speak and feel.

"Si, mi amor. For you."

Patiently, he moves my hips to find the right angle to touch me the way he knows will work, and to keep entering me a bit at a time. He knows exactly when to speed up and when to slow down, when to press deeper, and when to back off. I float on the edge of orgasm for what feels like days, with no interest in pushing or pulling anything along. I let myself sink into the ocean of pleasure I am experiencing. When my body begins to buckle with the intensity of it all, he holds me up. It's happening.

A cry from the bottom of my being rises out of my mouth. My body is white hot flames and the crack of electricity. But I am underwater, in another world. He holds me as I come and come and come. I don't think it will ever end and I have no interest in stopping it.

My body collapses, sprawled out on the bed, face down, unable to move. I can feel his hands on my back, soft kisses on my shoulder. He moves my hair to see my face. It takes everything I have to open my eyes and look at him. *I love you* fills my mind. I'm not sure if I say it out loud.

Marco looks at me and smiles. His face is in soft focus. "Are you happy?"

"No." His face changes. "I am ecstatic." The smile returns. "You are an amazing lover," I tell him, looking straight into his eyes.

"You are the source of all this, Monique. It's not me. It's you..."

When I wake up again, it's afternoon. A glance at the clock shocks me awake.

"Holy shit!"

"What's wrong?" I've frightened him awake.

"We overslept. Nora's ceremony is in a few hours. I have to go! She's going to kill me!"

"And maybe me too!" He springs out of bed and begins to gather my belongings. We are both dressed and out the door in minutes. Since it's Vegas, no one gives us a second look in our clearly disheveled states.

He insists on walking me to my room again. This time I gratefully accept. Every moment of this time together is enhanced. The way he holds my hand, the way he touches my back, the way he kisses me. The world has gotten brighter and more luminescent. I glide more than walk.

At my door, he says, "These next few hours without you will be like I am underwater, unable to breathe."

"Grow gills, darling. I'll see you very soon."

I watch him as he walks away, then tear myself away from that beautiful sight to enter the frenzy I'm sure is happening in my room.

The girls stop when I enter, saying nothing. They are looking for Marco.

"He's not here."

"Oh my God!! What happened? You look like a total mess, Nik. You did it, didn't you? The slutty dress worked?"

"Let her get a word in will you?" implores Nora.

"I love him." I can't believe I say it.

"No, sweetheart. You are just flooded with some biochemicals that feel like love. It's just lust."

"I love him, Nora. I'm serious. Something happened up there that I've never experienced. Never, in my 40 plus years as a woman. I don't even feel like the same person anymore."

"Oh my God Nik!" Lizzy exclaims. She has to sit down. I think she's crying.

Nora is unconvinced. "You just got properly fucked my dear. That's all. Ok? That's what a really good screw feels like. Don't confuse it with love. That's trouble in the making."

"Shut up Nora! Look at her? Doesn't she look different to you? I think you do, Nik. I think you look like a woman in love."

"Thank you sweetie. I feel amazing. Absolutely amazing. I swear to you something magical happened. I wish I could explain it."

Nora sighs deeply, exasperated by her romantic and foolhardy sisters. "No time for that now. It's a big day, if you happened to remember. Time to scrape your lover's stuff off your dirty body and get ready."

"Yes, boss," I say as I give her a hug.

"Love you," she says.

"Love you too."

"I guess you two will continue rummaging through my stuff while I'm in the shower?"

"Yup," they say in unison. "I might ask Claire to take me shopping. She did a really great job with you," Lizzy adds.

I return to find Lizzy doing Nora's makeup. They are such beautiful women. Sometimes it surprises me, even though I've been looking at them my whole life. Nora has dark eyes and hair, like our mother, and Lizzy is all gold and pink, with the blue eyes of Dad. With me in the middle, we make a perfect progression from one parent to another.

It's half an hour before we have to be downstairs. I am finishing up my own hair and makeup when the knock on the door comes. Thank God! Lizzy, aware of the surprise, jumps up to answer it.

She greets Sam with kisses on both cheeks. "Well that was nice!" he exclaims.

Nora must have heard a man's voice. "No more lovers in here, ladies. It's time to go!"

Sam opens the door wide and says, "No more lovers? Not even just one?"

Nora stands stunned and silent. This has happened so rarely in my life that I would have hardly recognized her expression, but it is becoming a habit in Vegas. Is she mad? Am I going to be in big trouble for arranging this? We all stand completely still, waiting for Nora to react. No one breathes.

"You're here," she says in disbelief.

"Of course I'm here sweetheart. Where else would I be?"

She runs to him and wraps her long body around his. "I can't believe you're here. How did this happen?"

Instead of answering, he kisses her. Passionately.

Lizzy and I are mesmerized by the scene of our sister expressing her adoration of her partner, and Sam reciprocating even more back at her. They are captivating to watch – beautiful, strong, completely enamored with each other. I can't help but wonder if Marco and I will ever have even a small piece of this. My heart beats faster as I think about seeing him in a few hours.

"Ok, you two. I need to finish getting dressed. Get out of here." They go off to Nora's room, hand in hand. It looks like I am safe.

Lizzy jumps up and down, "You did it, you did it!! Look Nik, did you see how happy she was? You really did it!"

"Yes, baby girl. *We* did good."

My mind is filled with my unusual sister as I get myself ready.

Nora reminds me of Mom, but in a strange way. Their personalities are nearly opposite, but they look exactly alike. And then there is the sadness that no one can name or fix. The one I share, but Danny and Lizzy seemed not to inherit.

I wonder what will fill that hole for Nora. I can't imagine that there is anything she wants that she doesn't already have, or have plans to achieve. It's no nonsense with her.

Sometimes, I see her stare off into space, like Mom used to, and like I still do. I understand the source of my sadness and yearning. At least I think I do. But Nora's is unclear. What is she dreaming of? What is she wishing for? And what can we do to help her get it?

I don't think it's an issue with her career. Nora loves what she does, although still blames our parents for forcing her into it. She's right. She was the good girl who did as she was told. But there is nothing else that she would have wanted to do, whether she admits it or not.

Nora even likes the politics of getting ahead in academia. She plays the game better than anyone I have ever seen, stopping at nothing short of success at every goal she creates. Thinking about it, I realize that's how she's always been with relationships as well. She has never been the victim. Always the victor.

Even after Lizzy and I are both ready, the conspicuous sounds continue from Nora's room.

"Nona, do you want us to wait for you?" we ask, cautiously, using our pet name for her, invented by Lizzy when Nora was too hard to say.

"No," she says breathlessly. "Don't wait!" We fall into the silliest, girly giggles, knowing exactly what's going on next door.

The two of us walk hand in hand, as we have been doing since we were kids, all the way to the ballroom. Lizzy updates me on her adventures with Esteban, describing the double wedding we are going to have, our matching dresses and how the wedding band will only play Salsa.

She has fallen hard for Esteban, although they are taking it slower, sexually, than Marco and me. She wants to know EVERYTHING that happened between us, and I oblige. Lizzy is the better listener of my two sisters, less inclined to analysis and more open-hearted.

When dinner is about to start, and we still don't see Nora or Sam, Lizzy and I smile at the thought of their surprise reunion. Both of us know we would be lucky to find as much love as they share, even in their unique way.

If Nora ever gave Sam any indication that he wouldn't get horribly rejected, he would be on his knee in a flash. They adore each other in this crazy meant-to-be way. Neither Lizzy nor I can imagine anyone else putting up with her. It is nothing short of miraculous.

The reunited couple arrives at the very last minute, and the awards ceremony goes beautifully. Nora is softened by Sam's surprise visit, so thrilled with us that we had arranged it, and comes off as beautiful, brilliant and charming. Her acceptance speech is funny, humble and she thanks each of us individually. She and Sam never stop beaming at each other.

Marco never leaves my mind. If I had to describe what happened to me that morning, that weekend, magical would be be the best word I could find. It has elements of fantasy and wonder and utter incredulity. But it's actually happening. At least I hope it is.

The audience rises to their feet for Nora, applauding wildly. Lizzy starts to whoop and others join her. My sister is one of the most difficult people I know, but there is no doubt that she is a rock star in her field. I am so immensely proud of her and want her to have everything her heart desires.

She hugs and kisses each of us two or three times.

"We love you Nona. And think you're the best!"

"I couldn't have asked for a better family."

Were those tears in her eyes?

A substantial crowd, eager for her attention, but polite enough to wait for her to finish up with her family, begins to form a circle around us.

"Nora, there's a crowd of people waiting to talk to you. Your adoring fans I believe," Sam informs her.

We wait as she effortlessly thanks and greets those awed by her presence. There is a small reception that we assume she wants to attend, but she says, "Let's go party at the wedding!"

Alright! We all agree. I had filled Sam in beforehand (and gotten him an invitation) so he is ready to go.

"Whatever you want, my love," he says to Nora. "You keep getting more and more amazing every minute I know you. However you want to be celebrated, sweetheart, you get it."

"I love you so much Sammy. Thank you for coming, even though I forbade you. This is the best surprise I have ever gotten."

"Nora the ice queen has soft spots. Who knew?" I can't help myself.

"Shall we?" she says to change the subject.

"Yay!!" squeals Lizzy. "Let's go get ready!"

The transition to wedding garb does not take long. We had all laid out our new fancy dresses, and just have to slip them on. A refresh of the face and hair completes the look. Lizzy insists we take pictures. We do make a rather stunning group - Sam in his tux, us in our gowns, surprisingly no legs showing, if you don't count the slits in our dresses.

Nora chose a deep violet, Lizzy is in bright pink and I wear a silvery blue silk sheath, that makes me look like a mermaid, they say. I like the compliment.

Our mouths drop as we walk into the first room, where the ceremony will be held. We have left Las Vegas and entered heaven, apparently.

Everything in the room is white and silver, so meticulously done that it's impossible to imagine that this was a hotel ballroom the day before. A flamenco guitarist fills the room with romance and each guest is more beautiful and elegant than the next. My concern about the formality of our dresses vanishes as I notice everyone in their finest, having taken 'black tie' very seriously.

Esteban sees us first, even with a room full of guests. He runs over to Lizzy, who is already hopping up and down, and swings her around as if she was a small child. He gives her a dramatic kiss on the mouth, and then bends down and gives her belly a gentle little kiss.

"How is my hot mama?"

She giggles. "Missed you, baby. This room is so beautiful, Stebby. Oh my God, I feel like I'm in heaven."

"Aah, not as beautiful as ours will be."

Nora, Sam and I freeze. Did he really just say that?? It would be just like our sprite of a sister to get engaged this weekend. The funny thing is that we don't worry about her. Well, not too much. She always ends up on the right side of things, even with this pregnancy. It's turning out to be the best thing that has ever happened to her. And maybe to all of us.

Sam puts his hand out. "Hello, Esteban. I am Sam, Lizzy's..."

"Brother-in-law," I offer.

"So nice to meet you. Your family has made this an extraordinary weekend. We are so honored that you wanted to share my brother's wedding with us."

"Oh, Esteban, it was so kind of you to invite us. This is absolutely amazing," I say.

"I am so rude, I am sorry," and he proceeds to kiss Nora and me, on both cheeks. Lizzy sticks her face out, waiting for her turn. He obliges.

"Are you ready for tonight?" he asks.

"Absolutely!"

Nora and I look at each other. What is happening tonight? Should we be worried?

They both look at us with mischief in their eyes. I have to admit they make a great couple, and his generosity with her pregnancy cements the deal with me. Even if they announce their engagement, I will be perfectly happy for them. Maybe even a little bit jealous.

"Excuse me, but I have to get back to my brother now. I just wanted to make sure you were all here."

"Can I come with you?" Lizzy asks tentatively.

"Of course, mi amor."

"Ok, we'll see you later," she says as he whisks her off.

"And where is your Romeo?" asks Sam.

"I don't..."

"Hello." Marco's voice comes from behind me. How long has he been standing there? I turn around slowly, knowing how amazing he is going to look and wanting to savor every moment.

He doesn't take his eyes off me as I face him. He reaches for my hand and kisses it lightly, still keeping his eyes locked on mine. He moves toward my cheek, I assume for a kiss, but instead whispers in my ear, "You take my breath away." And then he kisses my neck.

I want to swoon. I forget there is anyone else in the room, or that time and space exist. This man awakens something in me that is beyond desire. It's like the feeling a plug must have when it enters a socket.

He steps back, introduces himself to Sam and kisses Nora. Sam had studied some Spanish and is excited to use it tonight. He begins to speak, to Marco's delight.

"Now you are the only one, my darling, who needs to learn Spanish," he says as he squeezes my waist.

"Si senor," I say.

"Let me not forget the deep congratulations for our next Nobel Prize winner, Dr. Malone. How do you feel?"

Even listening to him speak makes me giddy.

"I don't know which was better... winning the award, or having my sisters and my partner conspire to have him here. It was all so wonderful, Marco. Thank you for asking."

"Of course," he says as he nods gently. "Would you like to meet some people?" he asks.

"Yes," I answer for all of us.

He leads us to the groom's family, which consists of about 150 people as far as I can tell. They each hug and kiss us, so pleased that we are there to celebrate their family's special occasion. Some of the English is quite good, some not so much. But everyone is welcoming and festive.

Sam and Nora get swept into the group, while Marco and I step away.

He stands in front of me and gives me a proper kiss. "Hello Bella. You made me wait too long."

"Hello darling. You missed me?"

"I've been trying to grow gills all day. Haven't quite gotten the hang of it yet."

He is so clever and funny. "Don't you have to take care of groomsmen things?"

"All I have to do is stand here and look at you. And maybe some other things a bit later."

I can't stop smiling, so he continues. "All I could think of today was you, and our wonderful morning. Was it a dream?"

"Yes, I think it must have been." I grow self-conscious and want to change the subject. "Thank you again for inviting us. We are so excited. And it seems that Esteban and Lizzy have something planned for later. Should I be concerned?"

"I wish I knew, but I wouldn't be worried. I will have to stand at the altar in a few minutes, but for now I am all yours. And I'd like to just parade you around the room for a bit."

"Am I just arm candy? Is that all I am to you?"

"Actually, I prefer my arm candy unwrapped."

"Hmmm. I'm afraid this will have to do for now."

"I suppose that's fine," he says mocking disappointment.

He introduces me to many more people, whose names I forget almost as soon as I hear them. He enthralls me as he moves through the room like royalty, so charming and elegant. How did I land this guy?

Esteban's other brother finds us, and lets Marco know they are starting.

He kisses me. "Until I can breathe again."

I can't move for a few moments, so entranced by him. I look up to find my family waving wildly at me, beckoning me to the seat they saved. I float the whole way over.

The wedding is as expected. The crowd gasps as the bride enters, looking like a cake topper - petite and perfect, bejeweled from head to toe and beaming like a little girl. Her husband-to-be cries as she walks towards him. Marco never stops looking at me, even as tears run down my cheeks. I don't mind one bit.

The wedding party leaves the room together, and the guests are ushered into the grand ballroom, which makes the ceremony hall look like a dingy closet. The decor moves from pristine white to a festival of colors. Everyone stands awe-struck, just for a moment, at the entryway, disbelieving the grandeur of what they are seeing. Thankfully the ushers keep people moving along.

The four of us exchange glances of disbelief.

"I can't believe we're here," mouths Lizzy.

"I know."

I am fully expecting to sit apart from Marco, understanding the tradition to have the entire wedding party together. But we enter and see a special table for the bride and groom, on an elevated stage, and no other specially designated table. This is a newfangled approach to weddings, I think, but I like it if I get to sit next to my man.

My thoughts are confirmed as we see our names on the table. The four of us, plus Marco, Esteban and Esteban's other brother and his wife, make up the table. The men have not yet arrived, so Sam is our token date for now.

But his attention is only for Nora. Her response to his arrival, which really could have gone either way, changed something in him. In them. Maybe all this love and lust around us is making all the relationships better. Not that they need any help, other than my sister being so demanding.

Even that thought makes me laugh, as I remember her puppy-dog face when she saw Sam in the room. And how they were so blatantly having sex, which my conservative sister would have never done with us so close by. Nora looks nothing short of blissful. I give myself a mental pat on the back for orchestrating this surprise. Not bad, Nik, I think to myself.

"Daydreaming again, Bella?" I hear to my right, and there he is. My beautiful man coming to be with me. Things could not be any better.

The evening passes too quickly. We eat and drink and dance to the wonderful band, playing a variety of Latin music and contemporary dance tunes. Sam is eager to show off the ballroom dance lessons he and Nora had taken, and Lizzy is happy to be swung around by her Prince Charming. I just want Marco to hold me, and that he does.

"I'm so sorry I had to rush off this morning," I tell him.

"Yes, that. It's ok, but only just this once." He flashes me that smile again.

"It was a bit frantic, and I didn't tell you what an incredible time I had last night. And this morning." We both smile remembering how we had woken up.

"The way you share yourself... how honest you are, even when it's hard... I want you to know that I don't take it lightly."

I don't know what to say. If only he knew how much I am concealing, how the rush of emotions I have around him nearly drowns me every time I see him. But I have never heard a man say the things he says to me and I want to let myself take it all in.

I let the part of me that wants to say, *He's too smooth! You're being played! Wake up!* make it's way out of my system. Then I close my eyes and feel him hold me.

"I feel the same way Marco. It's been wonderful, these days with you. Maybe I'm just having one of my famous daydreams?"

"Maybe we both are."

We are a well-matched couple, not only in the bedroom, but also on the dance floor. He is the perfect height for a partner, standing just half a head taller than me when I'm in heels. Our bodies fit together like puzzle pieces.

I realize that I don't worry about who's leading when I am with him. Being in charge all the time is exhausting, frankly, and this is a breath of fresh air. I release myself into his support, his guidance and give him my trust. This is working on and off the dance floor.

We spend most of the evening dancing, sometimes switching partners. My turn with Sam consists of us doing the most dramatic moves he can think of, steps that Nora would never let him get away with but ones he knows I'm willing to do. We laugh, strut, dip and spin.

"You look so happy, Nik. It's about time. And Marco can't stop looking at you, like he can't believe his eyes. You know you've totally got him, don't you?"

"Don't you think it's just too good to be true, Sammy? I mean he's too fucking perfect!"

"No, he's not perfect. But he might be really, really good. You deserve a man who is going to worship the ground you walk on, and also not let you get away with any shit. He might just be it."

"Don't say that Sammy. You're going to jinx everything!"

"Do you know who you remind me of?"

"You and Nora?"

"Nope. Even better. Claire and Peter."

Remembering my parents brings an ache to the center of my chest. It's impossible to not feel the hole they left or to imagine ever having a love affair like theirs. Could what he is saying be true?

"I miss them so much, Sammy. I can't really believe it…"

"Me too, Nik."

Sam knows the easiest way to distract me from my painful memories is to move my body, so he spins me around until I crumble with laughter. I miss my brother too, as if one of my limbs is gone, but Sam is a priceless gift in our family. The older brother we need. I give him a huge kiss and tell him how much I appreciate him coming.

"If not for you, sweet Nik."

We walk over to the table hand in hand, ready to sit and catch our breath. Marco and Lizzy are doing the twist on the dance floor, seeing who can go lowest. Despite her recent top-heaviness, she wins by quite a bit. Esteban and Nora, who stands about a head taller than him, appear to be having a serious conversation. I think she is interrogating him. Uh oh.

Sam and I have the same thought. "I better go save that poor young man before Nora castrates him," he offers. I can't help but laugh.

Marco sees me sitting by myself and comes over to grab me. He, Lizzy and I finish the song doing the 3-way bump. I can't remember having so much fun, feeling so free and loving a moment so dearly.

The announcement is made that the speeches are going to begin and we should take our seats. I am grateful for the break. A girl who lives in clogs and sandals has a hard time in the stilettos I'm pretending I can walk in.

"I would tell you that you can really move, but I've seen you at your best, and know that this is nothing."

"Marco!" I am concerned that someone has heard us, but am pleased to receive his compliment. "You better stop that, mister. We have to make it through this wedding."

"Do we?"

"Ughhh," I say feigning exasperation.

The speeches are heartfelt and beautiful. The fathers, both of whom speak, have the whole audience in tears. Apparently, they were childhood friends, reunited when their own children fell in love. I can't stop crying, which leaves Marco searching for tissues. I can see by the look on his face that he is touched and entertained by my emotional outpouring.

The speeches seem to be coming to a close when Esteban escorts Lizzy to the microphone. Nora and I look at each other, horrified. *What is that crazy girl going to do???*

"Hola mi amigos! Me llamo Elizabetta. Sorry but that's all the Spanish I know," she says with a sweet laugh. I don't blink or breathe, so surprised and concerned about what is happening. Everyone else seems ok, but I can't understand. Lizzy doesn't know any of these people. What is she doing up there?

"I just met the bride and groom recently, but I have to say they define love. This whole room is so full of love. I can't even describe it well. Maybe if I were a poet... but I'm not." Again one of Lizzy's signature giggles.

"Since I didn't know them that well, I had a hard time picking out a wedding gift, so I thought something else might work. When I was growing up, my sisters used to dance around the house and sing to me. It kept me from crying, I guess. Since they have shown me what love is I guess this song is for them too. And of course, my Stebby," and she blows Esteban a kiss.

She looks over at the band and gives them a 4-beat.

I can't believe this is happening. How did my sisters get such balls? Both of them. I must have gotten all their share of self-doubt.

Nora certainly received a less than normal share of insecurity. She had been sure of herself for as long as I can remember. When she and Sam met, it was as if they both fell under the same spell, simultaneously. There was no doubt that they would be together. She never appeared in any way uncertain that their feelings were real or that they were meant to be together.

In stark contrast, I've questioned every relationship I've ever had. Either thinking it was more than it was, or downplaying it if it was too intense. I never got it quite right. Will this be my time to know? Can I let go of all my mental gymnastics and use my instincts to experience this man? The magic of our night together fills my thoughts. This is indisputable.

All of me, why not take all of me.

Lizzy is singing our favorite song. I feel on the edge of tears again. Of all of us, she had inherited the most of mom's talent and the crowd can't believe what they are hearing. I can tell by the shocked delight on their faces. She could easily have pursued a professional career, but chose not to. No interest, I suppose.

But singing made her happy. And now it's making all these people happy too.

I glance over at Esteban, who I thought just might start crying, even before me. That guy has fallen for my sister, hook, line and sinker. Whatever her spell is, it landed on the right guy. Without knowing the words, he is even trying to sing along.

Nora and Sam are happily singing. She and I know this song forwards and backwards, and Sam has been the unwitting recipient of our many impromptu song and dance concerts.

The bride and groom rise to dance. They extend the song out, and Lizzy does some amazing jazz riffs. That girl is killing it.

I turn my gaze slowly to Marco. Instead of watching Lizzy, he is looking at me, smiling.

"This is your song. I remember from the other night. How wonderful."

"Yes, she's amazing, isn't she?"

"Yes. Both of your sisters are superstars. It must be hard."

I don't quite understand what he's saying and give him a quizzical look.

"It must be so hard to be as nearly perfect as they are, and still pale in comparison to you."

"Aren't you overflowing with compliments tonight?"

Marco tenderly sweeps the hair off my cheek and holds my face.

"I'm overflowing... yes... with something..."

His face is very serious.

"What is it?" I am terrified to ask but do anyway.

"You don't know? I thought you would."

I'm sure I stopped breathing. "Tell me... please."

"Yes. I will..."

The room erupts in applause, shocking both of us back into the moment. I can only imagine what he was about to say to me.

Marco, Esteban and the groom's other brothers invite everyone up to the penthouse after the reception. The guys had ordered a beautiful spread of snacks and champagne, expecting a significant crowd. At least 50 people, mostly family members, come up, and the party lasts until the wee hours. I am greeted as if I am the woman of the house, and I play the part. Marco and I are the consummate host and hostess.

His friends are wonderful to me, treating me as if I am already family, and forgiving my terrible Spanish. Apparently Marco had told them a bit about me, or the news had spread some other way, and there is a great deal of interest about me and my sisters.

Lizzy receives the most attention, after her superb performance, and loves every minute of it. She would have made a stupendous celebrity.

As the crowd begins to disperse, Lizzy disappears first - I'm sure she is absolutely exhausted. She tells me that she'll be staying a few extra days with Esteban. Then Nora lets me know that she and Sam are going to take a few extra days as well, maybe going up to the Grand Canyon or Hoover Dam. I wish I could have stayed too but I need to get home to my girls. I miss them so much. And Marco has to be in New York the rest of the week, so I would have been on my own anyway.

Nora and Sam slip out, followed by a slow trickle of the remaining guests. There are a few stragglers left as Marco takes my hand and leads me to the bedroom. We turn to face each other and he wraps his arms around me, holding me securely, swaying slightly as if the music was still playing.

"Thank you for coming with me tonight."

"Thank you for inviting me. Inviting all of us. It was a spectacular wedding."

"Because you were there."

"Marco, you say the most beautiful things. Sometimes I just can't believe my ears."

"I know you doubt me."

"I don't... that's not what I meant."

"You doubt what is happening here, between us. But what will you do when I have fallen in love with you?" Out of left field, this one stops my heart and freezes my body. "Will you believe me then?"

I bury my head in his neck, afraid to look at him. I can't speak.

"I know... it's not a question you can answer, is it?"

There's nothing I can say.

Marco steps behind me and begins to slowly unzip my dress. His hands, breath and mouth fill the spaces where the shimmery blue fabric falls away. I feel him moving down my body, until he is on his knees.

"That ass of yours, Bella… it's quite miraculous, you know."

"Glad you like it." I am surprised at my ability to be humorous considering all that is happening in my body.

Then he bites me. The sting mingles with the pleasure and I gasp. He is biting, licking and sucking me like a peach. "You are going to let me have it one day, aren't you?"

It was my intention to answer, but then he slips one of his fingers between my cheeks and begins to slide it along the length of me. A shiver covers my body.

"Marco…"

His fingers keep moving, eventually finding the warmest, wettest part of me. Just a few strokes dissolve me, but instead of lingering there, he begins to move his finger back toward my bottom, and pauses.

"You can have anything you want, Marco. Any part of me you want." He could have entered me right then, no part of me off limits to him.

"I'm so glad you said that, Bella." Instead of pressing the finger that's massaging my bottom, he removes his hand completely. I gasp again, because of its absence.

He takes my hips and spins me around, so that his face is now directly in front of my pussy. I begin to understand what he is referring to.

He runs his nose and lips down the small line of hair that ends at the opening of my lips. My knees buckle and I realize I'm still wearing my heels.

"I can't stand up, Marco."

"Yes…"

He moves the pooled fabric of my dress away from my ankles and begins to help me out of my shoes, kissing my feet and ankles. It gives me time to contemplate what he wants to do, the one thing I have stopped him from doing. Before now.

As he rises off his knees, and kisses me, I know I can't possibly resist him, no matter how self-conscious I feel.

We move to the bed like a couple approaching the shore, stepping in with anticipation, enjoying every wave and tickle of the warm water.

I lay myself down, knowing I am going to allow him where I previously had not. Beginning with my toes again, he kisses, licks and sucks nearly my entire body, until landing between my legs. My hands instinctively begin to push him away, even though my body is on fire for him.

"Let me taste you, amor. Let me please you…"

I release the tension in my arms, and his head descends. All I feel is the warmth of his breath, as he begins kissing me lightly. This is such a scary, vulnerable place for me – I hardly allow any men there – and I can't bear to look at him.

"I knew I would love how you smell, and how you taste. I imagined being with you, like this. Look at me, amor."

I open my eyes to see him smiling, with his eyes. His tongue is moving over me, slowly, like a child with an ice cream cone. I want so much to turn away, to stop the rush of what I'm feeling, but I can't. He continues to stroke me with his tongue, as he has done with his fingers. It's working. My body is responding, despite the situation in my mind.

He increases the pressure, and draws me strongly into his mouth. His tongue is inside me, and I can feel the brush of his whiskers. Then somehow his thumb replaces his tongue, and he is sucking on me tenderly and insistently. When his thumb begins to press upwards, from the inside, I know what the outcome will be.

"Marco! Oh my God!" Is it really possible that I am coming like this?

Not only possible, but undeniable. I find myself floating in some other world, unable to stop the waves of pleasure coursing through me.

He begins nuzzling the inside of my thighs as I recover, whispering 'Mi amor' between each kiss. I am incredulous when I feel the heat rise again. His slick thumb begins to move downward, now between my cheeks where he had begun this exploration.

"Do you like me touching you there?"

"Yes, Marco. I do." It is very hard to speak.

"Good," he says as gently presses the tip of his finger inside me.

My body, which he seems to know better than I do, has left my domain, and become his instrument. Layers of self-protection and shame dissolve under his hands and mouth.

And then he speaks the thoughts in my head.

"I want to be everywhere in your body at the same time."

He rises onto his knees, and wraps his arms around my waist to pull me up to him. When I reach down to wrap my hand around his cock, he closes his eyes and moans. He sits back onto his heels and places me astride him, as I had been the first night we stayed together. He expertly guides my body onto him, and moves me, with his arms around my back. The shock of feeling him enter me has not faded at all since the first time, and watching him try to manage his arousal nearly brings me to the edge again.

We are face-to-face, as bare as two people can be. There is nowhere I can look other than his loving eyes.

He stays present and patient as I find my way, battling my demons and letting my body experience him.

My moans grow louder, as he stays quiet and controlled, waiting for me.

"Tell me what I can do for you, Bella. What makes you happy?"

"You seem to already know what to do."

"Let yourself go, amor. Let yourself hear what my body is telling you."

We roll in an orgasm that moves back and forth between the two of us for minutes. When I want to break contact, he takes my face and makes me see him. This is an intimacy I have never experienced.

We fill the night with an entire sexual repertoire, finding each other over and over again. My previous difficulty with orgasms during sex fades into memory as he shows me how easy it can be.

He succeeds at demonstrating with his attention and passion what I can't hear in words. I trust him with my body, and now my heart. "I believe you," I whisper as he drifts off to sleep.

9

SHAKY GROUND

The morning is very busy, with both of us flying out, him to New York and me back home to San Francisco.

In the limo to the airport, a whisper of insecurity fills my body. Will this be the end?

I am compelled to ask. "What's next, Marco?"

"What's next... hmmm. Well, we spend these next few days apart, which will be terrible, then I return home on Friday and we... begin."

"We begin?"

"Yes, Monique. We begin the rest of our lives."

This is utterly romantic, but I'm looking for something much more concrete.

"Marco, perhaps it's too soon to make declarations, but I kind of need to know what... what's happening with us."

"What would you like to happen with us, Bella?"

"I should have known you would turn it around." I sigh. "OK, I'll go first. I want to see you, to be involved with you. I am... not interested in seeing anyone else." That was excruciatingly difficult.

Marco smiles. "That was hard for you. Thank you for doing it anyway."

I wish I could control how transparent I appear to be. "And you?"

"I am yours, Monique. There is no one else in my life. Just us."

I let myself exhale, happy that the moment is over.

The scene at the airport unfolds like a bad romantic comedy, neither of us wanting to let go of the other's hand. I spend the entire plane ride reliving my fantastical weekend. Could this really have happened? It does not seem possible.

It doesn't matter that I am alone - no sisters, no Marco - I am plenty busy with my thoughts. Landing home begins the frenzy of real life, and my arms are full with my beloved girls before I know it. They want to know everything, and I tell them some. They know me so well, I can't hide anything. But I do try to tone it down. I tell them about Nora's wonderful award ceremony and how we got invited to a wedding and how aunt Lizzy sang in front of everyone. I only mention that we had met some nice people – men – briefly.

Marco calls me as soon as he lands. "I miss you. I can't believe you were in my arms just a few hours ago and now we are thousands of miles apart. How are the girls?"

"Happy to see me. And I'm happy to see them too. We have a very full and busy week."

He has to run off to a dinner meeting, and we promise to talk tomorrow. "Buenos noches, mi amor."

We speak every day, sometimes several times a day. He asks about my progress in my restaurant endeavors and I ask about the big project he is working on in New York. I can't wait for him to get home over the weekend. We have a big date in the city all set up.

On Friday afternoon, right before he is supposed to get on the plane, Marco calls. He sounds terrible, and there is quite a bit of background noise. Like a train station. Or hospital.

"Where are you?"

"I'm sorry Monique, I won't be able to fly back tonight."

He sounds awful. As if he is in shock. "Are you ok?"

"Yes, but there's something here I have to take care of. I need to call you back later, ok?"

"Are the boys alright?" All these thoughts are running through my head: There has been an accident. He is in trouble. Something really, really bad has happened.

"Yes, they're fine. I'm sorry, I have to go now."

I don't hear from him for two days. The nightmare begins to take shape. He is a criminal, a drug lord maybe. He has a wife and children in New York that he neglected to tell me about. The stories come nonstop from my vivid imagination. I can't understand what would cause a man to completely disappear.

I feel like I'm losing my mind, filled with desperation and rage. There's a burning ache in the middle of my body where I anticipate his disappearance will live. All I hear in my head is, *You knew this was going to happen. It was all too good to be true. He's probably some sort of psychopath, on the run from the law, and you just got dumped.*

When I see his number pop up on my phone, I am honestly shocked. I am sure he had disappeared.

"Hello," I answer in as neutral a tone as I can muster.

"Mi amor. I'm sorry I haven't been able to call."

"What's going on, Marco?" Stay calm, stay calm.

"I can't really talk now. It's ok. Please don't worry."

"I wish you could tell me. I don't understand."

"I know. But I have to go now. I will try to get home in a few days. Then we can talk. Goodnight."

A few more days of stewing and I start to unravel. My sisters ask me what's going on and I can't even tell them. I have no idea, except that my magic carpet has been brutally pulled out from under me. I can hardly do anything but worry, projecting the worst possible scenarios.

It's two more days before I hear from him again. I try very hard not to sound crazed on the other end of the line.

"How are you doing?" I ask.

"I'm ok. I'm coming home tonight."

"Oh, good. Have a safe flight." I know he can hear the sharpness in my voice. Anger is the only thing holding me together at this point.

"I know you are angry darling. It's just... we will talk when I get home." I hear the flight announcement. "I will call you. Bye."

I can't tell if it's rage or despair fueling the breakdown I am destined to have. Something big is going on. I know it. I cry the rest of the night.

Part of me is afraid of falling asleep, of missing his call, but it's unnecessary. I don't hear from Marco again until the next afternoon.

If I ever see him again, I scream at no one, *I am going to let him know exactly how unacceptable this behavior is! I will not tolerate being treated like this!*

Part of me wants to believe that he will stroll into my house with a perfectly good excuse that will inspire my immediate forgiveness. The rest of me knows that something traumatic is about to happen. I prepare myself for the worst. I begin to justify the whole experience.

The story I rewrite sounds like this: It was a fabulously romantic and sexy affair. Like a summer fling, but shorter. I couldn't expect that someone would fall in love with me that quickly. What I was feeling was just lust. Just like Nora said. It had been a long time, and I just wasn't used to having sex. Great sex. It was all merely an excess of hormones causing my delusion, which would soon pass. He was not the man for me, especially if he had all this drama in his life. No, certainly not. I had more than enough drama already.

I tell myself I won't take his call, if it ever comes. I will make him wait and see how he likes it. Then he will know. Then he will come running back. The irrationality of my theory makes no difference to me.

There's no way I can keep myself from picking up the phone when his number appears.

"Can you meet me this afternoon? I can be at your house in 30 minutes."

"I can't. I have the girls."

"Please, Monique. I really need to see you. Just for a little while. Please."

I want to lash out and scream at him, all the awful things I've been thinking. I want to say *NO, I won't! I am so angry with you I don't think I could even look at your face!* Instead I say, "Fine. Meet me at the Colonial Cafe on Sutter. You said half an hour?" There is no way I'm going to let him in my house.

"Thank you my darling. I'll see you then."

Am I about to be dumped to my face? What do you wear to a dumping? Or am I about to find out that he is a serial killer? Time moved like cold molasses.

The girls are fine with my heading out for a little while. In fact, they are a bit frightened by my state of mind, and suggest I take a walk. Brilliant idea.

The cafe is only around the corner from me, but I walk for nearly the entire 30 minutes, talking to myself, getting stared at by the homeless people, and praying. Praying that the worst that I had imagined won't possibly come true. It can't.

Marco is already in the cafe when I arrive. His normally disheveled hair is especially so. He looks tired. And sad.

He pops up when he sees me and wraps his arms around me. Funny greeting for a dumping, I think. He looks at me and tries to kiss me, but I turn my cheek. He lingers there, and then crosses to the other. All the while searching my face, my frozen face, for any signs of what to expect.

"How are you?" he asks.

"Well... how I am is not really the subject of this meeting, is it?" Crushed glass is coming out of my throat. I can't help myself from trying to hurt him.

He drops his head and takes several deep breaths. It's killing me, waiting for him to say something.

"Are you going to tell me what's going on??" That sounds a bit hysterical, I have to admit. I am on the verge of bursting into flames.

"Yes." Then nothing again. For too long.

I close my eyes and begin to breathe. I have to keep control of myself. I am not going to show him my weakness, my hurt, my longing. I am not going to be afraid.

"There's a situation in New York that I haven't told you about. It's a bit strange, and hard to explain, and I was afraid you wouldn't understand. I know you've been feeling... uncertain about me... and us. I didn't know how you'd react over the phone. I was afraid..."

His pauses are killing me.

"But now something has happened. And you deserve to know." He runs his fingers through his hair, trying to get it out of his eyes. Then he reaches for my hand, which I pull away.

I can't let him touch me, as that will crack the whisper-thin container holding me together.

He looks at me to say something but I stare straight ahead. Cool and composed. Yes, that's what I am.

"A few years ago, I was in a relationship with someone. We were together for about 2 years. It was fairly serious, but we broke up. It was..."

"Why?"

"Why??" He seems to not understand my question.

"Why did you break up?"

"It was complicated. I knew how I wanted to feel but I didn't. Feel it. And she wanted to get more serious, have children. I knew I did not want to have children. With her. But we loved each other." He looks at me, perhaps regretting that statement. Did I flinch? I keep building up my container.

"We separated. It was very hard at first, but eventually we were on good terms again."

"How long ago was that?"

"The breakup?"

"Yes." You asshole, I want to say.

"Just over a year ago. And then, Carla, that's her name, got sick. She was diagnosed with bone cancer. And it was very bad. They said she only had a few months to live. She was very scared and asked for my help. I agreed.

So for the past several months, I've been spending time in New York, helping her with everything. And she had been doing remarkably well. Everyone thought she would recover. It was a real miracle. And then, this week, it got bad again. The cancer spread everywhere, even though we all thought she was doing so much better. Really it was getting much worse.

Carla's in the hospital and we don't know what will happen. It's not good."

I realize I am hearing about another human being's life and death situation, but all I can think of is one thing. "Did you become lovers again?"

"No. Not in that way."

"Not in that way??"

"We still had love for each other, have love, but it is not in that way... it's hard to describe."

"It sounds like you are having an intimate relationship with her."

He is getting frustrated at my responses. "Yes, Monique, nursing someone to their death is an intimate relationship. But it is not as you think."

This man magically knows exactly what will trigger me – betrayal, half-truths, infidelity. "How do you know what I think?" The seething and toxicity is spraying out of me. I am about to boil over.

"I don't," Marco says, the exhaustion spilling from his words and his body. "I don't know what you think. But I know you are angry. And perhaps you have a right to be. I just didn't know how to explain this to you. Do you see how complicated it is? And when we were in Vegas, I still thought that Carla would have a full recovery. Then the situation would no longer be an issue."

"So you would have never told me about it?" I am incredulous. The leaking grows faster and stronger.

"I just knew it would not go over well. I know you were scared about what was happening with us. This would be too much to handle."

"You have no idea what I can handle. I'm very strong you know!! And I REALLY don't like being treated like a child, or being lied to."

"I wasn't trying to do either of those things. And now I'm telling you everything, in the hope that you can just hear me. It's been very difficult..."

"You didn't go to New York on business at all, did you?"

"Monique, that's ridiculous. Listen, I don't know if I can handle any more but I have to go back in a couple of days. I just wanted you to know."

I take this as a personal offense. He should be groveling right now, begging me to take him back. Instead he's basically telling me to back off and let him do his thing with his dying girlfriend. I can't stand one more minute of this.

"You don't have to worry about me. I'm fine. You don't owe me anything either. Best of luck with your situation in New York. I hope Carla gets better. And don't worry about leaving. There's nothing more for you here."

I walk out the door, giving a brief glance back through the glass in the front of the cafe. Marco sits, mouth wide open, like a little boy who has just lost his puppy. I wish him nothing but suffering.

My phone begins to ring before I even walk in my front door. I don't answer it.

I kick myself that I didn't follow my first instinct that this man was too good to be true. He belongs in the same category as all the others – liars, cheaters, the ones who claimed to love me but never did.

I go into full lockdown, beginning a period of survival living, taking care of only what absolutely needs to be done, for myself, for my career, for my family. It's nose-to-the-grindstone time, with clear goals always in sight, and the fortress fortified. I will not let this destroy me.

I have to tell my sisters and Sam, so that they will know not to ask about Marco. They can't understand what happened, and I can't explain it. I forbid them from talking about it. I have a feeling that Lizzy is getting information from Esteban, but it doesn't matter. The subject is closed. The reality is that I am so ashamed at how I behaved in front of them, when we were in Las Vegas, like a lovesick teenager. It was embarrassing to completely lose myself like that. I will not let it happen again.

Marco continues to call and text and email, and I refuse to respond. My anger grows a life of its own as his messages accumulate on my phone. I am determined not to be felled by this monster again.

Until the nights, when I listen to his messages and cry myself to sleep. Every night. I think I will never reach the bottom of my sadness. I want to be swallowed whole by the darkness of what has been lost. I can find no way out of it or through it, so every night I just sit in it.

I listen to his false protestations of love for me and his insincere apologies for not telling me what was going on. He becomes more and more angry as I refuse to talk to him. His messages become more desperate and accusatory. And finally, there is resignation. He sounds desperately sad, and it makes me happy. I want him to feel even just the smallest part of the agony I've been through.

Time passes because it has to, not from any will on my part to move on. I go through the motions of my life, working day and night, taking care of my family, not taking care of myself. I feel empty and broken, like scraps of garbage floating on a dirty stream after a storm. My body carries me around, but other than that holds no use for me. It's cold, dry and empty. Maybe I look the same on the outside but it's just the shell of me. I feel both untethered and heavily weighted down. There is no place that doesn't hurt.

I relive our moments together over and over until I'm not sure if the memories are real or rewritten. I've been betrayed in the most poignant way for me and I can't let it go.

Looking at my own behavior, how irrational I was, makes me feel even worse. I only just met this man and spent a few days with him. That's all. It is not the ending of a 10 year marriage, or the loss of a beloved brother and parents, all of which I have survived. But this feels impossible to transcend. I can't decipher the intensity of my response.

The day finally comes when I'm brought face to face with something behind the impenetrable wall of my anger. With the help of a friend, my own bad behavior is revealed.

Emile did not ever spare me the truth, no matter how difficult, and this situation is no exception.

"Monique, you are behaving like an insane woman. You must put your head back on if you want to get anywhere."

"I've just been deeply hurt, Emile. Give me a break. I think I'm actually doing pretty damn well, considering."

"You are wrong. You are not doing well at all. You look like shit. Are you even sleeping?"

"Thanks a lot."

"What did this man do that was so wrong? He exhibited his humanity? He revealed that he is just as flawed as the rest of us? I don't understand why you won't even speak to him. I think you are being ridiculous. You are a grown woman, for god's sake. Start acting like it."

I am actually shocked by Emile's accusation. "I can't believe you're not supporting me here, Emile. Especially you. Especially after what happened with us."

"Marco is not me, Monique. Don't blend all your relationship experiences into this one situation. It sounds like he's actually trying to be a good guy. Don't punish him for the mistakes the rest of us have made."

I was so mired in my own suffering that my pettiness and cruelty were invisible to me. Until I hear what Emile is saying to me, then my anger turns into shame, and I realize how badly I behaved.

My disgrace, instead of creating an opening, keeps me even further from any possibility with Marco. My deep humiliation at making a situation that must have been grueling for him all about my own selfishness and insecurity now points to my current unworthiness. This is the final turn of the sword. I can't find my way around this new set of emotions, so I keep pretending he is a monster - a liar, cheat, manipulative, deceitful, terrible person. This story keeps me just within the line of complete collapse.

I have big work to do and can't afford to be taken down by another failed love affair. I have gathered more and more evidence that the world of the heart is not a safe place for me. It's best for me to stay in the world of logic and work, not feelings and emotions.

I can't ignore all the love around me and all these nearly perfect couples - Nora and Sam, now Lizzy and Esteban. I'm the only one who keeps failing, who can't find the love I want. Or singlehandedly destroys it.

But I do have my daughters. I tell myself that maybe that is the love I will experience in this lifetime. Maybe it isn't for me to be loved by a man in the way of my dreams because I receive so much love from my children.

Every day there's a new theory as to why I've ended up here, alone. With Marco, I experienced something completely different. It's nearly impossible to admit that now, as I try my best to discount the experience. I use my intellectual prowess to explain my feelings away. I've succeeded before in my life by turning off the feelings that were too much, or not right. I can do it again.

This goes on for weeks, until the tears become less frequent. I can tell the shell I had built is getting stronger. I'm making good progress in my work at the restaurant, feeling confident again. Marco's calls are less and less frequent, allowing the wound to heal. Or so I think.

I receive an invitation from Nora. I'm not strictly in the mood for a family dinner, but I suppose it beats sitting at home alone.

My social life has shrunken back to nothing after the debacle with Marco. Even thinking his name brings sharp pains to the base of my throat, as if I am being drowned. Still, being with my family could be nice. I know they are worried about me, and I want to show them that I am just fine.

I enter the house, tired and defensive. "Hey girls. I'm here."

I hear voices in the living room and head that way. Everyone is standing up, and as I scan the room I see an extra person. It's Marco.

It takes me a minute to compute what's going on.

"Monique..." he says softly.

"What the fuck? What are you doing here?" And then it dawns on me that my sisters have set me up. Again. They invited me over here to trick me into talking to him. Rage fills my body.

I look right at Nora. "Are you fucking kidding me? You are doing this to me again? I can't believe you." I turn around for the door. Sam and Marco run right behind me. The girls are too scared, I suppose.

Sam catches my arm first. "Listen here young lady," he says in that fatherly tone he sometimes adopts with us. "You aren't going anywhere. You are going to sit your ass down in there and listen to us. If you don't want to listen to Marco, you're going to listen to me. This has gone way too far and it's time that somebody did something about it. And that somebody is me."

He brings me back to the room and sits down next to me on the couch, holding my hand the whole time. Marco sits across from us, sandwiched between Nora and Lizzy.

"I'm so sorry Nik. I know this is really hard for you. We didn't want to make it so hard. But we didn't know what else to do. We just want you to be happy again. I want you to be happy. Like me," Lizzy speaks between deep sobs.

I am about to respond to Lizzy. Something angry and accusatory. Even insulting. The words are brewing, but Nora cuts me off. She isn't nearly as soft or kind as our baby sister.

"You can't keep running away every time something important happens to you, Monique. Your life will continue to be a series of things you did not do and did not try. You can be with him or not. It really doesn't have anything to do with me, with us. But you can't just hide and pretend that you're done. Just listen to him. That's all we're asking."

"Really Nora?? I thought it was just a good fuck!!"

I don't let her prepare a response as I continue.

"I know you're always so interested in demonstrating to me how shitty my life is, but you didn't have to do it in front of him. Since when did shame and ridicule become part of the plan to make someone's life better? I can't believe that you would do this to me. I've been taking care of myself all along here. You act as if I'm a child that constantly needs to be redirected. What gives you the right? I get to choose who I want to be with. Not you!!"

Nobody can speak. They know I'm right. But Sam is still holding me in my seat. I'm not allowed to go.

Softly, quietly, Marco speaks. "I asked them to help me. I begged them. I was desperate and didn't know what else to do. I know how close you are with your sisters and Sam. You trust them. And they trusted me. Maybe I could convince you too, if I had a chance. That's all I wanted Monique. A chance to be heard."

"They trust you because they don't really know you."

"Do you really believe that I am some sort of monster? That nothing was true?"

I can't answer that.

"Regardless, this is not about you. It's about my family's need to interfere in my life. And now to humiliate me."

"They are not here for YOU Monique! They are here for ME! I am the one who needed the help, whose life is in a shitpile right now. Don't you get it?"

"No, I don't get it."

"You wouldn't talk to me."

"That's because you're a fucking liar and I don't talk to liars."

Marco's head drops and the air leaves his body. "I'm sorry," he says just above a whisper.

Looking up, he says it a bit louder, "I'm sorry. I fucked up. I should have told you from the very beginning. But how? It's just such a strange situation and I was sure you wouldn't understand and I was right. I was so fucking scared Monique that you would do exactly what you did - walk away from me."

"I didn't walk away Marco. You abandoned me."

And there it is, the steaming hot mess of my fears, stinking up the middle of the room. My weakness, my neediness, my shame.

Sam looks at me understandingly, nods, then stands up. "We're leaving now," signaling to the girls. "We'll be upstairs. Please take all the time you need. We love you very much, Nik." He kisses my forehead. I watch them all shuffle out of the room, the only one looking back is Lizzy whose face is filled with pleading and despair.

"Please Nik. Just listen to him."

I have to look away from her, in order to stay calm.

We don't speak for several minutes. I feel a dam of emotion on the verge of breaking and I just need to keep the whole thing contained. I've shed so many tears over this man already. No more.

Marco stands up, walks around the table and sits next to me. Where Sam had been.

His voice shakes as he begins to speak. "When I saw you at the airport, just smiling and daydreaming, something happened to me. And then our weekend together was something out of a fairy tale. I still don't understand how it was all possible but I couldn't deny it. And I was going to do everything in my power to keep you around.

I didn't abandon you, but I know why you say that. You thought I lied to you, and chose someone else over you. I didn't handle the whole thing well. I know. It was stupid and I made this happen. This whole mess.

But I can't accept that you don't want to be with me. I think that's a lie. You're scared. I get it. But everything that happened between us was true. Everything I said to you about how I feel, is true."

I look up at him for the first time. Is he crying?

The dam breaks and all my composure washes away on a torrent of tears. All the hurt I've been trying to contain, just to keep going, floods out of me. I can't even think about composure. I am taken down and under.

He tries to put his arms around me, to comfort me, but I push him away. I can't get up, but I move myself to the far end of the couch away from him, put my head down and cry. I imagine he will just tire of this scene and leave. But he stays, inching himself closer to me.

I am so tired, drained by the act of holding up an empty body all this time without him. I am tired of pretending that everything is fine and I am just as competent and content as ever. I am tired of being the liar.

Marco puts his hand on my back, then slowly moves it around my waist and pulls me into him. I am too exhausted to resist. The tears keep flowing as he whispers, "I'm sorry. I'm sorry, Bella. I'm so sorry."

Although pain is still coursing through my body, I finally feel like I can breathe again. As if I have come out from dark cold water into the warmth and the light. It feels right to be in his arms. I can't deny it, even though I want to.

On a stream of tears, the words begin to flow. "It *was* like a fairy tale, Marco. How we met and the time we spent together. It was perfect. But nothing's perfect and all my ideas about it being too good to be true were right. You have this whole other life, with another woman, and you didn't tell me. You let me believe that... it was something else with us. But it isn't. You are with her in a very intimate way."

He moves me slightly away from him so he can look at my face. Shaking his head, he says, "I am with Carla because I promised. And I want to be there for her. I am with her as you would be with Emile, if he needed you."

"Emile and I did not have that kind of relationship."

"But you were lovers. And you love each other. What's the difference?"

Nora had said the same thing to me, and I hated hearing it now as much as I hated hearing it then.

"I told you about Emile, even though I didn't have to. My relationship with him was never a threat to you."

"YOU know that, but did I? All I could see was this man, who you call your best friend, who you had also been sleeping with. How do you think that sounds, from my perspective? Quite bad, right? But you know that it is different than how it sounds. And I trust you."

The sword enters and turns an inch. I have to close my eyes to absorb my foolishness. He's right. And yet when we were arguing he never threw that in my face, my blatant hypocrisy. Another quarter turn of the blade.

I need to go somewhere else. Away from this disgrace. "How is Carla doing?"

The question surprises him. "Things are not going well. But she is so strong. I don't really know what to expect, and the doctors don't have anything useful to say. How are you doing? How have you been?"

Strong Monique is finding her way back. I sit up straighter. "I'm ok. It's been very busy, with the magazine and the restaurant and the girls. We're really busy getting Lizzy ready for the baby, too. But that's been nice. Something to look forward to."

"And how are you?" he asks again.

His voice is like a truth serum. "It's been... very hard, Marco. I couldn't believe that my worst nightmares had come true. It was devastating. But I'm strong too, and I can just keep going."

"Without me?"

"Yes." I steady my voice as well as I can.

"I see."

Silence.

"What if I can't keep going without you? What if I just don't want to? What if I know that we are supposed to be together as clearly as I know this is my right hand?" His voice is cracking. "What can I do so you will believe me? How can I convince you that... I love you?"

My heart skips several beats.

"And I believe you love me too. I can feel it in your body when we are together. We are like magnets, Monique. Can't you feel it?"

"You don't know me. You don't know how I feel."

This makes him angry. He gets up off the couch and starts pacing.

"Maybe that's true. The way you're acting towards me now, certainly doesn't make sense. Are you really so scared of having someone know you and love you that you would push me away? You are foretelling your own fate."

"I didn't ask for this!" I yell up at him, across the room. I can hear myself speak, and I am disgusted by what is coming out of my mouth. When did I become such a victim? So pathetic?

He stops pacing. "Don't we all ask for love?"

"I don't know."

"Yes you do! Monique, don't you think you were part of this? That your heart was part of this? Am I that crazy that I imagined what was happening between us? If you were not asking for my love, what were you doing? Playing with me? Just having a bit of fun?"

"That's not fair."

"No, it's not. None of it is fair. We're not here because life is fair. We're here because we experienced something that happens so rarely among two human beings that it's nearly impossible. You make me feel like I made the whole thing up in my head. That it didn't really happen."

"Maybe it wasn't what we thought it was." The lies continue to come out of me. Am I testing him, or myself?

He sighs. "I can't make you love me. I can't make you be with me. You don't have to convince me how strong you are. I get it. You can do anything you want, you can have anything you want. What will you choose?"

I look at him. What will I choose? I know that there is still anger in my face. It probably hurts him to look at me, but he holds my gaze. He is strong, but I am stronger. I can make him suffer. I can make both of us suffer.

Or I can choose something else.

"I'm sorry," I say. His face completely changes. He is shocked.

"Why?" he asks.

"I got blindsided by the situation with Carla. I don't blame you for not telling me. All I've shown you is what a hysterical woman I am, from the very beginning. Marco, I feel so ashamed at so much of what I've done. I was out of my mind, maybe. But that's no excuse. I wanted to punish you for not choosing me. For choosing her. And no matter how much it hurt me, I was going to hurt you back.

I feel so vulnerable with you. And it scares the shit out of me. I made myself ripe for betrayal. Everything was surreal, and my reactions were not reasonable or rational. I just couldn't reconcile our time together in Vegas, then what happened when we came home.

It's all so humiliating. That's the best word I can think of. The situation with Carla was the perfect excuse."

"For what?"

"For me to convince myself that I couldn't possibly... that I had to leave before getting left. I just couldn't believe this would have a happy ending."

Marco listens and watches as he stands in front of the fireplace with his hands in his pockets. He looks like a confused little boy. My heart is melting.

"What do you want me to do, Monique? Just tell me. I'll do it."

"I don't know."

"Please tell me."

"I don't know, Marco."

"You don't know?? Really?" he is exasperated. For good reason.

"I want you to be honest with me." This is a good start.

"I can do that. Even when it's hard."

He begins to walk towards me. I stand up, not sure where the courage is coming from, but I say it – "I want you to love me." There it is. Out in the open. Finally.

Marco takes a long slow breath. I hope he is taking it in. "Do you want to love me back? Do you... love me back?"

"Yes." It has to come out. I can't stop it.

Neither of us moves. He puts his head in his hands. I can hardly look at him, so scared of what his reaction will be. I'm glad his face is hidden.

"My God," I hear him say. What does that mean? Did he not expect me to say yes? I want to dissolve into myself. Where can I hide?

"Please don't hide. Not now." I look up to find him watching me. I can't read what's on his face. Is it... sadness?

"I'm not hiding Marco. I'm talking to you."

"Why does it scare you so much?"

"Because it's overwhelming. And it's fast. And it's undeniable. Because I can pretend, but I can't hide."

Then it comes rushing out of him. "I am so in love with you it intoxicates me. I walk around in this new world where everything is different, better, because of you. I miss you when we are apart and don't want to let go of you when we're together. If you just let me love you, and I promise I will do the best I can, I won't give you anything to be afraid of."

I walk over to him. He takes my hands and puts them to his chest, over his heart. "If we need to start over, I can do that."

"We don't need to start over. I don't want to start over. I want to start from here."

His lips linger as he kisses my hands. "I was scared too... to tell you how I felt, because I knew it would scare you away. But I love you Monique. I love you..."

I kiss his lips as he is speaking. It feels like an eternity since I've felt his mouth on mine. The electricity is still there, just as I had remembered it. My body and my heart say yes to this man, loud and clear. My mind whispers, love him.

For a long time, we hold each other, afraid to move too much. I miss him so much I can feel it in my bones and my flesh, as if blood begins to flow again through my body. I want to stay there, in his arms, for the rest of eternity.

Footsteps, then a small voice. "Can we come down now?"

"Yes," we say simultaneously.

Lizzy sees us together and instantly starts to cry. "Oh Nik, you did it! I'm so happy for you. You belong together. Everyone can see that. I love you too, Marco. I'm so glad you asked me for help. You two apart is like the sun and moon not speaking or something."

"I'm not sure the sun and moon have a speaking relationship, Lizzy," from the voice of logic.

"Nora!!" scolds Sam.

"Ok, ok. Just a joke. Who's hungry?"

I'm not hungry for food. I'm so full of the certainty of my being with Marco. Everything he said is right. Everything. I was too much of a coward to say, but know it's true.

"You two might not be hungry now. But you should eat anyway. You might need a little cooling down," Nora says with a raised eyebrow.

"Yes, ma'am," Marco says obediently. Everyone laughs.

It's nice to be together. All of us, except for Esteban, who is still in Los Angeles. I know Lizzy is going to see him in a few days and she can't contain her excitement. I keep waiting to hear that they've eloped, but they are actually taking it relatively slow. Relatively for Lizzy, our ultra-romantic sister.

Unlike my impetuous plunge, they have not even slept together, and are waiting until after the baby is born. I can't help but admire the maturity of their relationship. I am supposed to be the big sister, but I've acted the most childishly.

We sit at the dinner table for hours, enjoying each other. Marco touches me the entire time, and doesn't let me out of his sight. Even when I have to go to the bathroom, he wants to come in. I refuse. I can tell he is seriously trying to make up for what happened.

We don't talk about Carla, or what we are going to do about it, but I know we can work it out. Together. That is a conversation for another day. Tonight is about enjoying our reunion.

My sisters and Sam each take me to the side to apologize for what they did. They felt desperate and sad for me, I know. My anger has dissolved, and I apologize for making it so hard for everyone. They promise no more interventions, and I promise no more cause.

"Are you guys going to stay over?" asks Lizzy excitedly. "I am! You definitely should. Then Nik can make us her famous breakfast in the morning."

"Oh really?"

"I think it sounds like a great idea. It's late and who wants to drive all the way back into the city?" says Marco.

"Yay!" Lizzy exclaims.

"I suppose," I say pretending resignation. "Sam, did you stock the fridge?"

"What do you think? I knew you were coming."

"I really wish you guys weren't so sneaky. It doesn't suit you," I say with a smirk.

We settle back into the living room, the men build a fire and Nora whips up some hot chocolate with and without fortification.

As the evening comes to a close, the reality of the night brings back a nervousness I haven't felt in so long. I lead Marco up to the guest room, the one I always stay in, my body shaking as I think of being with him. I didn't think I would ever feel him next to me again.

"Are you cold?"

"No. Not really. I think I'm nervous."

"Me too."

I'm shocked to hear him say that. I was so absorbed in what a big deal this was for me, that I forgot that he was going through the same thing.

"I missed you so much Monique. I felt like a broken man. And I didn't know how things were going to go tonight. I didn't know if you would ever forgive me, or want to be with me again."

"I didn't either. Thank you for not giving up. I know it would have been so easy to walk away from me – all my messiness, and craziness. To imagine yourself so much better off. I wouldn't have blamed you."

"I wish you could see what I see, Nik. I don't see a crazy lady. I see someone whose heart is so big that sometimes it feels like too much. But it's not too much for me. I want all of you, remember?"

It's going to take me a long time to unravel what happened tonight. How I cracked the armor around my heart and began to feel again. Maybe it will remain a mystery, like the magic that happened in Las Vegas.

I wrap my arms around him. "Let's go to bed."

"I thought you'd never ask."

We move as if for the first time, tentative and watchful. Marco speaks to me the whole time, making sure I am ok. When he enters me, we both stop.

"Monique, my love, I need you to trust me, ok? I know I screwed up, and gave you reason to doubt me, but I promise I will do everything to make sure that never happens again. But I need to know you're with me. I don't think I could take…"

"I know, Marco. I know." I can hardly stand to see the sadness on his face. "I love you. And I trust you. With everything I have."

He begins to move gently, and the shell breaks irreversibly. *Don't be the idiot that ever lets this man go again,* I hear inside my head.

We are clumsy and silly and in love. There is nothing perfect about our lovemaking other than that we are sharing the experience together. We fit together like magnets, just like he said that day at the pool, so long ago.

I thought I would be the first one up, but I find Sam already in the kitchen, making coffee.

"Good morning sleeping beauty. Feeling better?"

"Yes, thanks for asking. And next time you want to stage an intervention as an excuse for my sister to let you stay over, please use somebody else's life."

"Clearly, I'll have to. I don't anticipate you're going to have any family-worthy drama anymore. But knowing you..."

"You're such an asshole."

"That's why you love me."

"Somebody's got to."

"Yes, yes, I suppose that's true."

I do adore Sam. How straight he is with us and how kind.

"Stop daydreaming, missy. You know how your family gets when they're hungry. You better start cooking."

"Ay ay, cap'n. Are you on toast duty, as usual?"

"You got it."

Sam loves to cook and we make a great pair in the kitchen. He is also one of my biggest fans.

The next set of footsteps - is it Nora or Marco? Definitely not Lizzy as she will easily sleep until the afternoon.

It's Marco.

"Good morning darling," he says after a lingering kiss. "Sam, how are you?"

"Very well, my friend. Very well. And you?"

"Aaaah, I believe somebody turned the world right-side up last night. Everything is perfect."

I can't help but smile. He always has the most beautiful things to say.

I know I still have some healing to do, and some forgiving of myself and Marco. I behaved abominably. I accused him of all sorts of monstrosities but it was me who had grown the fangs and the tail.

I get back to my cooking, but find it hard to participate in the festivities. Everyone is so happy that Marco and I have found our way back together. I am too, even though I know we have a long way to go. *I* have a long way to go."

"Another amazing breakfast, sis!"

"This is amazing. I really love the eggs today, Nik."

"Thanks guys. It's my pleasure."

Marco beams at me. Perhaps he thought I would have never forgiven him. How foolish I was, to let my perceived rejection taint everything. Thank goodness for his persistence, and my family's intrusiveness. I feel immensely grateful.

10

CALM AFTER THE STORM

Marco and I begin again, this time more carefully. Over the weeks that pass, we reveal our lives to each other, discovering everything left out in our fast and furious love affair. I happily spend time at his beautiful apartment, when he is in town, and try not to lose my mind when he is in New York.

He invites me to accompany him, to meet his boys, but I can't get myself to go. The idea of meeting Carla, the poor dying woman on whom I had wished such ill will, is horrifying to me. Apparently, she is doing very poorly and will not make it much longer. She is back at home, with the little family she has, and is as comfortable as could be expected.

Marco is infinitely patient with me. I don't know how he does it. I am unreasonable and demanding and sometimes just plain crazy. He lets me be however I need to be and just holds me. I understand why Carla wants him. He is the perfect companion in times of stress or hardship.

Life seems to take a turn for the better, in so many ways. Crisis no longer feels imminent and I settle in to a period of contentment. It's an ordinary day when I get the call from my sister.

"Hey No..."

"Listen. I'm on my way to the hospital with Lizzy. She's bleeding. Get here, ok?"

"What?"

"Just get here!"

The phone goes quiet. I can't believe what I just heard. Lizzy had not been feeling well all week. We figured a bit of rest would do her good. What is happening?

I grab my headset, get in the car and start making calls. Jeff needs to pick up the girls. I have to call the restaurant about not being able to make my shift. And I call Marco.

"It might be nothing. These things happen all the time, and it turns out just fine." Am I trying to convince myself?

"I'll be right there." I knew he would come, and I want him to.

Nora texts me that they have gone to the emergency room, so I stop there first. Nora is standing at the reception desk, speaking to the attendant.

She grabs my hand when she sees me. There is fear in her eyes.

"They're taking her up to a room."

"What's going on, Nora? What happened?"

"It was so bad, Nik. She was bleeding all over the place. I have never seen that much blood. This can't be good, Nik."

"You can come with me," says a man in blue scrubs.

We clutch each other's hands as we are led to the main part of the hospital.

"You can go up this elevator to the 14th floor. There is a waiting room just opposite the elevators. Wait there until the doctors are done examining her."

"Thank you."

Neither one of us can speak during the ride up, perhaps imagining the worst and not wanting to share it. The whole situation with Lizzy and the baby has been so strange. How the father is such a jerk and yet she wanted to keep the baby, and then meeting Esteban who was more than happy to help Lizzy raise the baby. I don't know what to think now, except that I need my baby sister to be fine. To be perfectly fine.

Nora and I hold each other, until Sam joins us. It feels like hours pass, and none of us can speak. We all jump as the doctor enters the waiting area.

"Can we see her?" I ask.

"Shortly." He looks quite serious.

"What's going on?" Nora asks.

"Your sister is having a miscarriage. It appears there were some serious congenital issues with the fetus, and it spontaneously miscarried. Because it is relatively late in her pregnancy, it can be quite traumatic, physically and emotionally."

"Oh my God!"

"She lost a great deal of blood, so we are going to keep her overnight for close observation."

"Is she in pain?" I ask hesitatingly.

"There might be mild discomfort, but no pain. It's important that she stay calm. This can be a very emotional event, but for her own health, she needs to stay calm."

I hate doctors. What a stupid fucking thing to say to someone. You've just lost your baby, maybe almost your life, but the important thing is to stay calm. I want to hit that man.

Sam takes us both by the hand and leads us toward Lizzy's room. Before we enter, he looks straight at me. "Nik, we don't know how she's going to react. We want to be there for her, ok?"

"Ok." I don't want to understand why he is saying that only to me, but I know. I need to be strong for my baby sister.

We open the door slowly, to find Lizzy typing into her phone, and crying softly. She smiles when she sees us.

"Hi guys."

"Sweet girl... how are you feeling?"

"Been better. But ok, I guess. It doesn't hurt that much, when you have a miscarriage."

I catch my breath, close my eyes and compose myself. I start to stroke her soft golden hair.

"Esteban is about to get on a plane. I told him he didn't have to come up, but he insisted."

"He loves you honey. Of course he's going to come."

"I appreciate you all coming too. I'm glad you're here."

"Of course we would be." I don't know what else to say.

"I guess it wasn't my time to be a mommy yet, huh?"

Nora begins to sob. We all look over in shock.

"Nona, don't cry. It's ok. Really it is. I'm sad I didn't get to meet this baby, but he was very special. He taught me so many things in his short little life. Maybe he'll come back again, when I'm more ready."

"Sweetie, you would have made the best mommy we've ever seen. You **will** be the best mommy. You didn't do anything wrong."

"I guess. But Mom always told us we have to know when it's right. With a man. And I knew it wasn't right with Mike. He was an asshole. And maybe this baby didn't want to have an asshole for a father."

"Maybe," is all I can say. My baby sister is the craziest, zaniest and in some ways the least mature of us, but sometimes she is like a wise old woman. She can see a world that most of us don't have access to, except when we see with our hearts. Anyone else might have been inconsolable, but she sees something completely different in this horrible experience. She is like a creature from another world.

We all stand quietly around the bed and hold Lizzy and each other. No one moves when the door opens.

"Hola Elizabetta."

It's Marco.

I turn to him and all my composure is gone. I step aside so he can move in towards the bed. He leans over and gives her two kisses. Her favorite double-cheek kisses. He speaks to her in Spanish. "Como esta?"

Lizzy has been furiously studying Spanish, to surprise Esteban.

"Bien. Et tu?"

"Muy male. I am worried about my sweet little sister. Is she feeling ok?"

"I am ok Marco, really. It doesn't hurt nearly at all. And all my family is here. And Esteban is coming too."

"I know. I will go get him from the airport. He is trying to get here as fast as he can."

"I know. I wish he wouldn't worry. I'm going to be just fine."

"We know, sweetheart. We know."

We all sit with Lizzy through the rest of the afternoon and night, taking turns crying, and soothing each other. We sing together and watch terrible movies on the hospital TV.

When Esteban arrives, he looks as if he's been crying. He goes straight to Lizzy and holds her. "Mi amor, mi amor," he says.

The rest of us step out to the waiting room to give them some time together. What must he think? I wonder. This is not even his child, but he has taken Lizzy and the baby as a set. He was more than willing to raise another man's child, just to be with the woman he loved. He is a hero.

After some time, I go in to check on them, and find them in the tiny bed together, sleeping. Esteban has himself wrapped completely around her, as if he was her protective blanket.

We all stay in the waiting room in various stages of sleep and wake. I keep trying to tell Marco that he doesn't have to stay, but he insists, and I'm glad to have him here.

We wake up with stiff necks and sore backs, but happy to have stayed. Lizzy teases us all for looking so disheveled. We are told that she can go home later that day, but will have to come back for more tests in a day or two.

She decides to stay at Nora's, after we all insist, and we promise to take turns nursing her back to health. She swears that she is just fine. Esteban never leaves her side for the entire week. Anytime Lizzy wants a drink of water or a snack or even to just walk around, he is there, waiting on her hand and foot.

We have a small ceremony for Baby Boy, and Esteban proposes to Lizzy as soon as she recovers. She is as healthy, physically and emotionally, as I have ever known her to be, and she is deliriously happy with her new love.

My ideas about an elopement end up completely wrong as they plan an extravagant Las Vegas wedding. Lizzy gives up her San Francisco apartment to move in with Nora, but spends more and more time in Los Angeles with Esteban. We expect to hear that she is moving down there anytime, but I believe she does not want to tell us quite yet. Her work requires her to be in town every week or so, which keeps her close enough to us.

I begin to settle back into normal life, when I am reminded about events happening in threes.

Carla dies. Marco needs me to be there for him, and I am. I let go of all the ridiculousness and decide to just love my man and appreciate this amazing thing he did for another human being. He insists I come to the funeral with him, which I really don't want to do. I think it will be too awkward, but he wants me there and I go.

It is a beautiful ceremony, serene and intimate. Marco's eulogy is remarkable and I understand why she needed him. I am so proud of him, even as he breaks down in my arms. If I can help from thinking about how odd it is to be at my boyfriend's ex-girlfriend's funeral, then it will be fine. I will be fine.

He is appreciative that I came, perhaps not believing that I would agree. I had spent so much time hating him for what he did, all I needed to do was be there for him, and that would have changed everything. Would have prevented those weeks of absolute misery we both experienced. If only I could turn back time.

Instead, I have to let go of that terrified woman who creates her own tragedies. I have to be the woman who is strong enough to step fully into her dreams. I have to trust in what my heart has been telling me all long.

I return home to find that I've been fired and replaced at the restaurant, event number three. I wasn't aware you could be fired from a job you did for free, but apparently it is possible. Between the time I took off to take care of Lizzy and the time to go to NY, it was apparently deemed unacceptable.

Perhaps I had learned all I needed to from that place. Perhaps it's time to put myself out there for real, doing what I am meant to do. I buckle down to create the next step in my journey back to my beloved kitchen. This time, on my terms.

I realize that I have been holding back on one aspect of my relationship with Marco, and it is finally time to turn the page on the painful events of the past few weeks, and move into a new intimacy. I hadn't yet introduced Marco to my girls. I am highly protective of them and never want to bring anything into their lives that could cause them any pain. They'd heard about Marco, mostly from their aunts, and were dying to meet him, but I stalled. I'd been stepping very carefully, but Marco eventually got his invitation to my house, to meet my children. We were all excessively nervous.

We plan a full evening of cooking and movies. The girls sense this is important, but being so young, don't strictly know what to think. This is a big step for me, bringing a man home. I haven't allowed any other men since their father into this part of my life, except for Emile, who they know as a friend and only a friend.

Marco arrives fully loaded with gifts and goodies. Not having girls of his own, he is clearly unsure of himself, so he overdoes it. The girls, of course, are terribly impressed. Who says the key to a girl's heart is not shiny things?

Attempting to draw attention away from the extravagant gifts, I move us all to the kitchen to finish our dinner preparations. The girls are thrilled that I've fallen in love with cooking again. Food has become a source of joy to me again, as opposed to a place of constant soreness. The life of a successful chef might be (temporarily) behind me, but feeding my family with love is again an important part of my life.

The girls have always been adept in the kitchen and love to take responsibility for their parts of the menu. I put them in charge of guiding Marco.

The kitchen is small, so we have to work together. With the three of us, we've figured out a system, but an extra set of hands, and a large unfamiliar body, throws us off a bit. There's quite a bit of bumping into each other and dropping things, which leads to great hilarity.

Claire and Lola remind me so much of Nora and me when we were young. Claire was born serious, and very, very talented. She is a natural leader and gets things done. Lola is my wild child - extremely emotive and eloquent, with an uncanny ability to see into people's souls. Her insights border on the psychic and I often wonder if she has some connection to a magical world we can't see.

Claire takes on the task of directing Marco in the kitchen, and freely critiquing his work. Lola plies him with a nonstop stream of questions, relevance and appropriateness notwithstanding. He obliges both of them.

Every now and then I stop and watch them. I had no doubt they would get along brilliantly, but was not quite sure what that would look like. I can see that he is a very good father. He is natural, easy, relaxed and honest. He never speaks down to them or tries to ingratiate himself. When Claire gets a little too bossy, he tells her. When he needs a break from Lola's questions in order to concentrate on his preparations, he tells her.

I am impressed. He looks over at me and mouths, I love you. He takes every opportunity to brush against me, or touch my arm. We both pretend that the girls don't notice.

The meal is imperfect in its preparation, but perfect in its enjoyment. Everyone offers to clean up afterwards, which is a great surprise to me. The girls are then put in charge of setting up the movie, which leaves Marco and me alone, for the first time, in the kitchen. With my hands busy in the sink, he takes my shoulders and kisses me passionately. The combination of this man, in my house, with my girls in the other room makes everything more exciting. And scary.

We settle in on the sprawled out floor cushions, at first a bit tentative about who is going to sit where. Normally the girls would each lay on one of my shoulders, but no one wants to leave Marco out, so we create a new foursome shape. I snuggle under Marco's arm, and the girls fit themselves in around us. He holds them as if they are his own. My heart is warmed.

I had chosen a comedy, so as not to have to cry in front of everyone... again. Whenever he can, Marco sneaks in a kiss or a whisper.

Although the girls are too excited to sleep, having a new visitor over, I force the issue. I promise a great breakfast, which everyone expects anyway, and usher them off to bed. And then things get awkward. Or maybe just for me.

We had agreed that he would stay the night, but now that it's time to bring him to my bedroom, I feel uneasy. I don't have men over, and now one is spending the night. I wonder how much the girls understand about what that means. I know Claire has a good idea about what happens between men and women. What does she think? Will Lola be her normal inquisitive self and ask us about it in the morning? I am feeling embarrassed already.

I'm not sure I can be intimate with him, concerned about the girls so close by. What if they want to come into the room, which they often do?

"It's ok, darling. Don't worry. The girls will be fine. And maybe, so will we."

He reads my mind again. "I know. It just feels strange to have you here. Doesn't it feel strange to you?"

"Not really. Maybe just a bit, because I can feel your nervousness. I don't want to make you feel uncomfortable. Do you want me to sleep in the other room?"

"Don't be ridiculous. I just... I don't know..."

"Didn't the girls see you and Jeff being affectionate?"

"No. Actually no one did, because it so rarely happened. Especially after the girls were born. That's pathetic, right?"

"No, not pathetic. Truthful. Now don't you want them to have a good example of what it looks like, an adult relationship? I mean one that's not on TV."

"They do, from their father. He and his girlfriend have been serious for some time, and I know that she lives there most of the time. I'm not worried about that so much..."

"So what are you worried about?"

"I guess I haven't really had to split my attention before. I want to make sure that I'm taking care of everyone."

"But what if I want to take care of you? Will you let me?"

"If you insist." We both laugh, but I feel the seriousness of his statement. Will I let him take care of me? Can I allow myself such an unlikely extravagance?

We lay down in my bed, breathing together. There is a softness to my desire, but I can tell he is waiting for me to make the first move. He is being respectful about my concern around the girls. It feels like the first time having a man at your parent's house. Something sacred is being transformed. Not necessarily broken, but evolved.

I want him to love me, here, in the bedroom that has never experienced that event. I begin to kiss his neck, and my hands explore his body. I can feel him relax, and he responds to me quickly. I slide my body on top of his and crouch above him. He holds me and kisses me, not forcing anything to happen. But the heat builds quickly for me, and I want to be with him. I slide him inside me, and he moans. I close my eyes and let him move the both of us.

I expected to feel differently, less engaged, with him here, but our bodies connect as deeply as ever. We are quiet and gentle and still as electric. I raise and lower my body on his, and he guides me with his hands. I know he likes looking up at me in this way, and I hold his gaze.

"Mi amor, mi amor."

"Are you happy?" I ask him.

"Happy is not the word for this. Thank you for bringing me into your family. Your life."

"I love you Marco. Thank you for letting me love you."

I move more vigorously and his excitement builds. I sense his climax approaching. He always wants to wait for me to orgasm first, and sometimes I won't give him the chance. Tonight, he is being insistent on waiting for me, and tilts me forward, so that I can feel the extra friction of rubbing against him. With infinite patience, he takes me to my climax, then turns me onto my side as my body softens.

"You loving me is more than I could have ever dreamed of," he says.

He holds me so tightly while he comes, I think I may break. I love that feeling, of his power and strength, even in complete surrender. He tries to keep quiet for the sake of the girls, but I can feel the vibration of his moan through his chest.

"Now this bed has been officially christened."

Marco laughs, understanding my joke.

"The first of many."

We sleep easily, although I wake up many times just to look at him, in my room, in my bed. I can't believe my eyes, then slip back to my dreams.

*   *   *

The next six months pass like a sweet sigh. All the turbulence and drama of the prior two months dissolves, leaving only the petals of some especially beautiful blossoms.

Jeff's girlfriend gives birth to a beautiful baby boy, and they decide to get married. I am honestly happy for them, and the girls, although initially hoping for a baby sister, find their new brother adorable.

The professional awards continue to accumulate for Nora and she and Sam even talk about combining households. After almost 20 years of being in a committed relationship, this is a big deal for them.

I begin a new job working in a downtown restaurant catering to the corporate lunch set. Most restaurants like that do boringly ordinary food, but this place prides itself on creatively healthful cuisine, with a famous name chef at the helm. Since he is there infrequently, I have relatively free reign as Executive Sous Chef. I can't have imagined a better situation that lets me be home with my girls in the afternoons and be in the kitchen during the day.

Marco and I settle into our own rhythm, spending several days a week together, either at his place or mine with the girls. I travel to New York more and more frequently with him to visit his sons who are kind and welcoming. We feel like a family to me.

11

ARGENTINA

We plan a trip to Argentina, for his father's 75th birthday celebration. Although Marco is both Italian and Argentinian, his closest family members are all in South America. I intensify my efforts to learn Spanish, afraid I won't be able to communicate with his large family, and nervous about making a good impression. Apparently, he has not brought a woman home for a very long time, and my visit is anxiously anticipated.

I can't believe it's possible, but I love him even more, as time goes on. The more we are together, the more we enjoy each other's company, which is such a change from my history. Being with Marco is making me a better person. He teaches me how to trust by being a perfect steward of my heart. I let the scars from our past issues soften and heal.

We are both nervous before the trip. My anxiety revolves around meeting the family, and I assume Marco's revolves around the same. He comes from a very large, very prominent, family and they have apparently not enjoyed some of the previous women he has brought home. I find this out through Lizzy, who gets the scoop from Esteban.

On the one hand, this man is an important part of my life. On the other, his family is thousands of miles away, so if we don't get along, it won't be the end of the world. Still, I want people to like me (one of my many flaws) and I want *these* people to like me.

During the long plane ride, I can see Marco is distracted. He says he is thinking about the plans for his father's party, and the logistics of doing everything he wants to do while we are down there. His boys will be joining us in a few days, too.

I fall asleep on the long ride from the airport, and wake up to find we are parked in front of a huge, white estate. Maybe even a villa. Certainly one of the biggest houses I have ever seen. Marco's father Andres, one of the most successful real estate developers in South America, lives a grand life, which I learned from Lizzy.

Since it is so early in the morning, Marco assures me no one will be awake, and I will have plenty of time to rest and freshen up before the introductions begin.

Andres opens the door, wearing a beautiful silk dressing robe. For a moment, he reminds me of Hugh Heffner, but much better looking.

Marco is surprised to see him there, at the door. Without pause, Andres wraps his arms around his son and holds him tightly. "My darling son, you are here, you are here." Then he kisses him firmly on both cheeks and looks him square in the face.

"Life is good, I see," Andres says with a sly smile.

"Papa, this is Monique. Monique, this is Andres, my father, who is never up at this hour."

I completely forget myself and begin to put my hand out to shake his. Not sure if he notices or not, but he takes me by the shoulders, and kisses me just as firmly on both cheeks.

"Buenos dias, senor Gonzales."

"Now I see why my son never comes to see me anymore." His English is flawless.

Uh-oh, I think. In trouble already.

"I would not leave your side either. How wonderful to meet you, finally," he adds.

"Can we go in, Papa?" We are still standing at the entryway.

"What a beautiful house," I say as I try to take it all in. It is a cross between an old European castle and a funky modern museum.

"Gracias. It's home," he says with clearly false modesty.

"Why are you awake, Papa?"

"I wanted to be the one to greet you. And Monique. There is some coffee, and maybe even some pastries. I know it has been a long flight."

"It was very easy," I say. "Thank you."

"Leave your things here. Martino will bring them up shortly."

He escorts us to an impeccable sitting room, where a tea and coffee service fit for the queen is laid out. I look at Marco in disbelief. He had greatly under-represented his family's stature. This is the big leagues.

"Thank you, Papa. You are looking very well, too."

"All is well, Marco. I continue to be the luckiest man alive."

Andres begins to serve us. Marco informs him that I don't drink coffee, and he sends for a woman called Isabella to bring some lemons. I am embarrassed, already looking needy and peculiar.

"I hear this is very good for you, the hot water and lemon. Is that true?" This man is truly charming.

"Yes, that's what they say. Let's hope they're right!" Everyone laughs, and my discomfort fades.

Marco and his father begin to speak, very quickly, in Spanish. They are talking about the boys, I believe, and the business. I am following fairly well, but it's taking some serious concentration, which in my fatigued state, is not plentiful.

"I am so sorry, my dear. How rude of us to exclude you. We must speak only English from now on."

"It's ok, Mr. Gonzales. I have been studying Spanish..."

"She's doing very well," adds Marco.

"I can usually keep up fairly well, but maybe not this morning, in my... state."

"Yes, you two must be very tired. We can finish up here, then you can go upstairs to rest. I am so pleased that you came. It means very much to me. And please stop calling me Mr. Gonzales. It makes me feel very old..."

"Don't worry Papa. No one would ever think such a thing."

"Thank you, Andres. It is really lovely to be here," I add.

When we arrive in the room, the luggage has been carefully arranged at the foot of the bed.

"This is like an opulent hotel," I say to Marco.

"Yes... it's a bit over the top, isn't it?"

"Not really. It is amazing though. Very beautiful."

He wraps his arms around me and begins to kiss my neck. "*You are very beautiful.*"

I move his head and begin to kiss him, softly at first, then passionately. My feelings of fatigue begin to melt under the heat of my excitement.

"Are you still tired?" I ask.

"No," he says as he presses our hips together. "Muy caliente," he says, using a euphemism for being turned on.

We begin to peel each other's clothes off, our mouths never losing contact. I am surprised to find myself so aroused, after being so exhausted just a few minutes ago. The intensity of our connection continues to build the longer we are together. Gone are the days of my frigidity and my insecurity. My sex vixen is running the show these days.

We never make it to the bed. As we are undressing, I find myself against a huge armoire. Marco lifts one of my legs and enters me. Things move very quickly for both of us. As he begins to slow down, trying to cool things down, I say, "Please don't stop." The intensity is intoxicating, and him taking me in this way is unbelievably exciting.

Our bodies know exactly what to do, even though standing up is a rare position for us. I can feel the electricity begin to fill my body and my legs buckle. Marco holds me up, while still moving against me, up and down. I press one of my hands against the wall to steady myself, and keep from collapsing.

"Marco!" I exclaim.

"Si, amor, si," he encourages me.

A deep groan comes through my body, out of my mouth. I try to muffle myself by keeping my face against his body, but the sound fills the room. I am barely aware of how he does it, but he picks me up and lays me on the bed and slides himself back inside me.

The heat rises again. I really love having him on top of me, maybe more than anything else. I don't care how traditional it is - missionary is very productive for us.

"It's your turn, my love."

"I think it's still your turn," he jokes with me.

I grab his bottom and pull him deep into me. He moans and I know it won't be long before he climaxes.

I hold his face to mine as the pulses of pleasure beat through his body. That feeling never gets old for me. Marco is such a generous and attentive lover, anytime I can give him pleasure is delightful for me.

He lays still for a few moments, and I think he may have fallen asleep. I gently stroke his back.

"Thank you for being here with me," he says. "You don't know how much it means to me."

"Almost as much as it means to me that you invited me."

"Well, none of the others could make it," he says jokingly.

I give him a playful slap on the bottom and we laugh as we move under the covers.

"Is it nap time?" I ask.

"Absolutely."

Marco is still sleeping when I wake up, so I decide to quietly slip out and take a shower. I walk around the room in awe, admiring every piece of furniture and art. His family is wealthy, that's undoubtedly true, but they are also incredibly tasteful, which does not always go together. The mixtures of colors and textures, the use of light and open space, all make for a sophisticated, yet inviting space.

The bathroom is a showpiece, with an open shower area in the middle of the large room. I think it's certainly larger than some of the apartments of my youth.

I luxuriate in the hot shower. It feels so good, removing the grime of traveling, and waking me up. I'm enjoying the water raining down on me, when I notice that Marco has come into the bathroom. I'm not sure how long he has been watching me - I didn't hear him enter. The broad grin on his face lets me know he has been enjoying the show.

He opens the door and asks, "May I join you?"

He's already stepped in before I say yes.

"Good morning, darling," I greet him.

"Yes. Yes it is."

I move him under the spray of the showerhead and let him enjoy the hot water. Then I take the soap and begin to wash his body. I know he loves my touching him like this, and it isn't so bad for me either.

It still takes my breath away to look at him, such a perfect specimen of a man. Lean, muscular, and perfectly proportional. I often imagine him being carved out of a piece of light caramel granite. He is athletic by nature, and prioritizes staying fit and healthy, but is not preoccupied or obsessed with his body. If I looked like that, I'd be preening all the time.

I love the shape of his broad shoulders and strong chest. I am always amazed at how soft his skin is and stroking him is one of my favorite activities.

My hands move around his body, under the premise of cleaning him. I linger in some areas longer than others, and he grows excited. So do I. Although we just made love, we are still aroused.

I move him towards the cedar bench, and whisper, "Sit down," in his ear. He obliges. I kneel facing him, and take him into my mouth. The water and the heat make him even more delicious.

I don't get to linger there as he pulls my body up to him. My legs straddle him as I lower myself slowly onto him. The slickness of our bodies creates a wonderful range of movement and pleasure. I feel especially playful and cannot stop giggling, almost as if I am drunk. I'm enjoying my lover in the shower of his father's immense house. I can't help but laugh.

We find our way to a passionate ending, but emerge waterlogged and pruney. He keeps looking at me as if I have lost my mind, and maybe I have. I feel as free as I have ever been, and as connected to another human being as I ever thought possible.

"Did I mention how much I love you?" I say as I run the soft towel on his beautiful body.

"Not yet," he says teasingly.

"As much as all the marble in this house."

We both laugh.

The rest of the day is filled with party planning and family introductions. Everyone is kind and gracious. I feel welcomed at every turn. We plan to have dinner at his sister's house, in a nearby town, that night. She has a large family, and Marco warns me to expect a bit more chaos and frenzy than his father's pristine environment. I am excited to see what a female Marco is like.

Dinner goes flawlessly, other than my numerous failed attempts at Spanish. Everyone is patient and understanding, and the children all want to practice their English, all five of them. Marco's sister is an artist, like their mother, and their house reminds me of something from Gaudi, out of Barcelona. It is fun and light and sometimes downright silly.

Carolina's husband is a regular comedian, a soft round man with a belly that laughs with him. He is utterly charming and a consummate host. I can tell she runs things, and he is the entertainment, quite divergent from the typical Argentinian patriarchy.

She and I find ourselves alone in the hallway near the end of dinner. She stops to look at me, as if something is on the tip of her tongue.

"Carolina, thank you so much for dinner. I love your family! It was so nice to have this night with you, without all the others around."

"You are quite welcome, Monique. We have been dying to meet you for too long. You know, I was supposed to be at the wedding, where Marco met you."

Although the details aren't quite right, I do not feel any need to correct her. "Yes, it would have been wonderful to meet you then. But I was so infatuated with Marco that I'm not sure I would have given you proper attention." We both smile.

"Marco and I have always been very close. We are almost like twins."

"Yes, I can see that. And he always talks about you with such love."

"He has been through so much in his life, all I want is for him to be happy."

I'm not sure where this is going, and I am starting to feel a bit uneasy.

She continues. "I know that you two had a difficult time not too long ago."

I gulp. "Yes. I was very foolish. And scared. The way we fell in love seemed to be too good to be true. I panicked. I feel very ashamed about what happened."

"He does seem like Prince Charming, doesn't he?"

"Yes. He does."

"And you are his princess."

I have no idea how to respond to that.

"I know you love him. I can see it in your eyes."

"Yes, I do Carolina. More than I could ever describe. I want him to feel that every moment of his life."

"Aaaaah, I think he does. I know he does, in fact."

She is silent for an uncomfortable amount of time.

I want to cut the tension. "Perhaps we should get back to the rest..."

"What I want to say to you, Monique, is thank you. Marco has always been my hero, and it has broken my heart to see him alone, or in relationships that did not make him happy. You have brought back the man I knew, Monique. The one whose heart is so full you can feel it in his presence. He deserves the best. I think you have given that to each other. And I am grateful. For you."

Tears press against my throat. This unexpected outpouring of love is too much for my emotional sensibilities. All I can do is wrap my arms around her.

"Thank you, Carolina. Thank you."

We walk back to chaos in the dining room, with the children climbing all over Marco, and the men having a heated discussion in Spanish.

Carolina admonishes them. "No politics at the table."

"Yes, of course, my darling," her jolly husband responds. I think he was losing the argument.

Although they beg us to stay, Marco insists that we have to return to his father's house tonight. There is so much to do, he claims. I don't really understand, but I let him make the decision. When I remember the talk his sister and I had in the hallway, I think I might cry. She gives me a very warm hug as we leave, and says, "We are so glad you are here. It is wonderful!"

I fall asleep nearly as soon as my head hits the pillow. The day has taken a lot out of me. I don't have to work nearly as hard as I thought to impress everyone, but I am still on my absolute best behavior. Keeping up with the Spanish also fatigues my brain quite a bit.

I wake up in the middle of the night to Marco, watching me.

"What are you doing sweetheart?"

"Just watching you. It's better than dreaming."

"You should sleep. It's going to be a busy day."

"I know. My head is just full. Actually I'm very happy. With you here, and my whole family going to be in one place. I can't really believe it yet."

"Are we picking up the boys in the morning?"

"No, they'll take the car. And they'll probably go straight to bed. My dad is taking them riding in the afternoon, with their cousins, which they will love."

"Ok, love, can I do something to help you sleep?"

"Just lay here with me. That's all I need. That's all I ever need."

"That and a nice clean shower every now and then," I joke, referring to our morning's activities.

"I'm so glad you enjoy being with me in that way. It is... wonderful. And not something I'm used to."

"Really? I don't think there exists a woman who could resist you. Don't you know you are the sexiest man alive?"

"Ha, ha. I'm not sure everyone received that memo. But I'm glad you think so. And the feeling is mutual, you know."

"You think I'm the sexiest man alive? Why thank you."

"Maybe the funniest one too."

"Yes, that I am. Now let's sleep." I snuggle under his arm and wrap myself around him. Both my heart and my body love sleeping in this position. Sometimes we find ourselves tangled in the morning, but it's worth it.

The knock on the door wakes us up.

"Senor Gonzales. The boys are here!"

It's the maid, excited.

"Thank you, Isabella."

"I'll go down to greet them, and rescue them from my father's planned interrogation. Stay up here if you like, darling. Get some rest."

"No, I want to come down and see them."

We put on our robes, and skip down the stairs to see Andres holding each of the boys by the arm.

"Marco, you didn't tell me what men they had become."

"Papa!" They run to their father with hugs and kisses. I even get a few myself. Andres can't stop beaming. Grandpa is clearly very proud.

"How was your flight, boys?" Marco asks.

"Other than Pablo thinking he had a chance with the flight attendant..." ribs Diego.

"Shut up! You're just jealous that I got extra dessert."

"Boys," interrupts an amused Marco. "Don't you want to rest?"

"Actually, we're ok, Papa. We slept some on the plane."

"Between the fights?" asks Andres.

We all smile. "Glad you're here, guys. Maybe eat something and then lay low. You know how much energy you'll need for riding later."

"Are we still riding later Grandpa?? We can't wait!"

All the men begin speaking in Spanish, hyperspeed. I know I can't keep up.

"I think I'll go for a run," I whisper to Marco.

"I'm sorry amor, are we leaving you out?"

"Not at all, sweetheart. I want you to catch up. All this male Gonzales energy, in one room, is too much for a sensitive gal like myself." I often joked that if Marco did not behave I would happily take one of his gorgeous sons instead. I was only mostly joking. They are stunning men.

It feels good to get outside before the sun rises too high. Winter at home, it is summer here and the temperatures are scorching. Two of the grounds-people vehemently offer to accompany me, not understanding I am trying to exercise. I do my best to explain, but am not sure I do.

When I return from my run, the downstairs is much quieter. I think the boys finally succumbed to fatigue and went upstairs. But where are the older men?

A trip to the kitchen for some water uncovers the elder, having a heated discussion over the menu for the day, I believe. He stops his conversation to offer me about 10 different things to eat and drink. "Just water," I repeat, as kindly as possible. He doesn't know where Marco is. Maybe working upstairs.

A search in our room comes up empty, so I start peaking my head into random rooms. I find Marco in the library, nestled into a huge, brown chair, smiling down at an oversized book. He is looking at pictures.

"There you are!" I say.

"I thought you had enough of this craziness and ran away from me."

"Not yet, love. Not yet. What are you looking at?"

"Come sit with me and I'll show you."

"But I'm so sweaty."

"My favorite," he says with a grin. It's true. Marco loves the way I smell, no matter what. Sometimes I do believe he is intoxicated with me, as he claims to be.

"Is that your mother?"

"Yes."

"My God, she was so beautiful. Wow. She looks like Marilyn Monroe."

"Funny for an Italian girl, yes? Her family is from the North, and they look more Swiss than Italian."

"Either way, she is stunning."

As he flips through pages of the album, I recognize some of the pictures from his house, and some of the people I have already met. The pictures of him as a child are adorable.

Marco tells me about all the people I will be meeting at the party tomorrow night. It's going to be a huge affair and I will likely forget most of the names, but it's wonderful getting a tour of his extensive family. I feel included.

"What a wonderful family you have." I mean it.

"They are your family too," he says. I look at him oddly and he turns away. I wonder if he is offended. I hope not.

"Let me go get cleaned up, my love. What is the plan for the day?"

"I told them we'd like a late breakfast, then we have a couple of visits, and... another appointment this afternoon."

"An appointment?" That sounds strange to me, especially since he stumbles on the words.

"Yes, yes, don't worry. Nothing you need to worry about."

"Ok," I say, a bit confused as I head towards our room.

We eat in the small room adjacent to the kitchen. Everything is delicious. "I'd love to get my hands on that kitchen," I say over breakfast. It's a showpiece.

"I'm not sure that will happen darling. There is not a lot of acceptance for people crossing lines here."

"You mean because the help will not like me in their territory, or because the family will not like me consorting with the help?"

"Well, neither, I believe. But maybe we can arrange something." We prepare ourselves for the start of the day and Marco lets me know we will likely be out all day. There is a dinner for only the immediate family tonight, as the kickoff for the major celebration tomorrow. The house is buzzing with preparations and I'm not unhappy to be heading out away from the frenzy. Andres and the boys are leaving for the riding grounds shortly.

At each house we visit, we meet more aunts, uncles and cousins, who each want to feed us more than the ones before. I have to learn more ways to say *no thank you* if I want to fit in my dress for tomorrow.

The family visits end and off we go to the secret appointment. I can sense that Marco is distracted, agitated even, but he won't say why. I wonder if I've done something to embarrass him or myself. I keep thinking that everything is going so well, and don't understand his strange mood.

Is he worried? Or upset? I try hard not to take it personally.

I snuggle closer to him and whisper, "Hey."

"Hi darling."

"Have I told you today how much I love you?"

His body softens. "Tell me again."

With small kisses between each word, I say, "I... love... you... so... much."

"Don't stop, ok?"

What a strange response, I think. "I wouldn't think of it."

We are quiet for the rest of the ride through the congested city, but he never lets go of my hand, holding it a bit tighter than usual. He gives our driver some instructions which I don't understand as he pulls over near what looks like a small patch of green in between buildings. We are in a very busy part of the city. Downtown perhaps.

"Where are we, Marco?"

"I want to show you something, ok?"

"Of course."

We walk into what I initially think is a small grassy area, and then am surprised as I round the corner and realize it is an idyllic urban retreat. Tucked away between skyscrapers, with an amazing view of the Buenos Aires skyline. I can't believe what I'm seeing, and watch with my eyes and mouth wide open.

"This is incredible, Marco. What is it?"

"It's one of our many secret parks. My father's office used to be in that building," pointing to a shiny skyscraper, "and I would come down here as a child after school, waiting for him. I sat on the bench over there and watched the buildings and the people all day. I would look down here," pointing me toward the skyline, "and draw what I saw. It's where I first realized that I loved structures and shapes, not in an artistic way like my mother, but in a practical way. I wanted to build things."

"Let's sit down," he says as he guides me to the bench.

"This is so beautiful Marco. Thank you for bringing me here."

"It's an important place for me. When I think of my childhood, I think of this bench, right here."

I am incredibly touched.

"When I got a little older I started noticing the people a bit more than the buildings. The businessmen - it was only men back then - the families, the couples. That's when I started thinking about what I wanted my life to be. I imagined my career, how successful I would be, my family, who I would love."

"And who was that?"

"Well, back then it was Linda Sanchez, the tallest girl in the eighth grade."

"Did she love you back?"

"Unfortunately, no. She had eyes for my brother, who spent much more time wooing girls than... staring at buildings."

Despite the mention of his brother, I can see he is relaxing a bit. I am so happy that he is sharing this part of his life with me. Marco is quiet for a moment, and then starts again, this time more seriously.

"I didn't really know what love was, back then, but I knew what it looked like from all those hours watching the couples hold hands, kiss, and gaze at each other. I imagined what it must feel like, inside, to be that way, and I wanted it. I wanted to feel that."

He looks out in the distance, probably remembering those scenes.

"I've made so many mistakes in my life, Monique... done so many things wrong. But somehow it all worked out. I got everything I dreamed of, nearly. I've had such a wonderful life... the boys, my career, almost everything."

He's smiling. "But that feeling... what I imagined those couples must be feeling... that one was... elusive. I thought I knew what it would be like, to be in love, but it was never as I imagined. Never that feeling..."

"Not even with Carla?" I wonder if it's awkward for me to bring up his late ex-girlfriend.

He shakes his head. "We had great affection for each other, and so much in common. I think we confused friendship and familiarity for some other kind of love. It just wasn't... it."

I remember him describing the relationship with Anna in similar terms.

"I more or less decided that what I imagined wasn't real. That I had just made it up."

I don't know where this conversation is going, but I feel anxious, all of a sudden. And sad about Marco's story.

"Then one day I saw this woman, this stunning woman, daydreaming at the San Francisco airport." He looks at me and smiles. "And then we spent the most magical days of my life, up to that point, together. And then she left me..."

I don't like where this is going. "And then you found her again," I add.

"It was during that time that I realized that that feeling I had imagined, so long ago, here on this bench - it was real. I did not just make it up. It was real and I was feeling it. Or I was feeling the absence of it. I knew, Monique that I just wanted to love you. I knew that I would have to find a way to be with you. I knew I wanted to spend the rest of my days loving you."

My breath begins to quicken and tears press against my throat. I can't take my eyes off him, although it's adding to my rising emotions. *Oh my God* fills thoughts.

"I can't explain what happened, or what is happening, with us. It is our fairytale, amor. You have made this boy's dreams come true. Being with you is everything I dreamed being in love would be."

Marco slides off the bench and gets on one knee. I can't process what I am seeing. He releases one of my hands to reach into his pocket, removing a tiny red silk pouch, then uses his other hand to open it. Out comes a magnificent diamond ring. He turns to face me. I am crying and having trouble breathing.

"Monique, you are the love of my life. I don't want to spend any of it without you. Would you marry me?"

I feel paralyzed. My head is spinning and my heart is pounding and I can't move or speak. My mouth is probably wide open. In my head all I hear is, oh my God, oh my God...

He tilts my chin so that I can see him. When our eyes meet, the whole world dissolves. It's just us, me and my beloved, the man who captured my heart in a way I have never experienced. I want nothing more than to be with this man... forever.

"Yes," I say between sobs. "Yes, of course. My God, Marco. I can't believe..."

I stop speaking as he slides the ring on my finger. In the sunlight it looks enormous, with a hint of pink. It fits perfectly, in every way.

"Oh my God," I keep repeating. Marco moves back onto the bench, takes my face in his hands and kisses me. I melt under the heat of his mouth. My head is still spinning but I stay connected to him, to keep me from floating off into space.

I move slightly away, to take a breath, and I can't tell if it's my tears on his face, or his. He's smiling that smile that captured me in the very beginning.

'Did you plan all this?" is all I could say.

"Yes, for quite some time. I wasn't sure if there was going to be too much going on during this trip, this weekend, but I couldn't wait any longer. This ring was burning a hole in my pocket."

"It's so beautiful, Marco. It's perfect."

"I'm glad you like it."

"Of course I like it. I love it. Because it came from you. I can't believe it..." I try to compose myself. "I love you so much Marco. I didn't need any of this, you know. You had my heart, regardless."

"I never thought of myself as old-fashioned. But I wanted to do this. I want our bond to be formal. And as serious as my commitment to you."

"I don't doubt you, darling. I don't doubt us."

When he kisses me again, I feel the relief in his body. I've put him through more than he deserved. To make this man happy is all I want right now.

"How long were you planning this?"

"About 5 and a half weeks. More or less." We both laugh.

"It sounds so trite, but it's true. You've made my dreams come true, Monique. I'm going to do everything I can to make yours come true too."

"You already have, darling. I never thought I would find love like this... I didn't believe it was possible for me either. And then you appeared, like a mirage. You have changed everything about what I see for my life. I... I'm just in shock right now. Sorry I'm being incoherent."

"You're never incoherent. Or maybe we both are."

"We belong together, I guess."

"You guess?"

"I love you, Marco," I stroke his face, "and I promise to keep loving you for as long as I breathe. And maybe a few lifetimes after that as well."

"Just a few?"

"Well it's already been several thousand! How many more do you want?"

"All of them. I want all of them."

With that, we both start singing my favorite song. We sit on the park bench, singing and kissing and watching the buildings and the people.

As we walk back to the car, hand in hand, I say, "Look, darling. Now you are one of the people you were watching as a boy. Maybe we will inspire someone to believe in their hearts too."

"I hope so."

We hardly speak on the way back to the house. I'm processing what just happened, and hyper-aware of the new sensation on my ring finger. Empty for so long, and now full.

Marco holds me. He is so much more relaxed, and I now understand why he had been acting so strangely. It must have been nearly impossible to keep it all in for so long. His thoughtfulness never ceases to amaze me.

I'm hoping that the house will be quiet, or everyone will be busy preparing for the family dinner so that we can have some time alone. As soon as the door opens, however, I hear the shouts of congratulations and get handed a glass of champagne. Andres is the first to greet me.

"Welcome to the family, my dear. We are very happy to have you." He squeezes me so tightly I can hardly breathe, then kisses me square on the mouth. I don't have time to be startled because the next family members have their arms around me. I keep trying to look over at Marco, to find out how he told everyone, but he is swarmed as well.

It looks like everyone has arrived early for the dinner, or maybe the dinner was just a ruse. I'm not sure of anything at this point.

The boys each take me aside to welcome me to the family.

"We are so pleased you and Papa are together. We love you, Monique. Thanks for making Papa so happy. It's been a long time."

"I love you two very much, and can't believe I am lucky enough to be part of your family." They wrap around me like my daughters do, even though they are both taller than me.

The crowd moves into the ballroom, the music starts and the party begins. I finally make my way to Marco. "What is all this?"

"Didn't you realize how much my family loves parties?"

"How did they know?" I ask, suspiciously.

"I only told my father, my brother and sister, and the boys. I guess they told everyone else. I didn't know they were going to do all this. I was hoping we could sneak upstairs..."

"Me too," I say with a wink. "I have an engagement present for you..."

He is definitely intrigued. "Do you think they will miss us?"

"Yes! You'll have to wait until later, I suppose."

"I am dying with anticipation..."

"Break it up lovebirds! Plenty of time for that on the honeymoon," says his cousin Juan. "When is the wedding?"

"We haven't gotten that far yet. Don't worry, you're all invited, of course," I say.

"Does that mean no romantic getaway to Bali, then?" Marco asks.

"We can do both, can't we?"

"You mean I get to marry you more than once? That's the most brilliant thing I've ever heard."

"And by the way Juan, there's going to be A LOT of this for... forever!" He then gives me the biggest, most dramatic, kiss he can. He nearly knocks me off my feet, which is how it feels to be with him. Hovering slightly off the ground. I can't recall a time when I was happier. Then I remember...

"Oh my God! I have to call home, and tell everyone. I do have to sneak off."

"Yes, I'll let them know where we're going."

Marco tells his father, who is busy dancing like a man half his age. "Si, si..."

We can't believe our luck, to be allowed to leave so easily, and skip up the stairs.

I dial my girls first. This will be the more complicated conversation, I think. How will I explain to them that I am marrying someone other than their father? I know they love Marco, but will they find it strange? Will they feel betrayed?

"I'm calling the girls now, sweetheart. I hope they will be ok."

"I think they will. Just call."

I remember that their father is planning his own wedding. That might make things a bit easier to explain.

"Hi Mama!" They are on speaker.

"Hi sweet cakes. How are my love bugs?"

"We're great... watching a movie. What are you doing?"

"Well, I have some news..."

"Did you say yes?! Did you Mama? We both thought you would! Did you???" Both girls are speaking at once, over each other.

I'm confused about what I'm hearing. How did they know? I look over at Marco, who is grinning sheepishly.

"Yes, girls. I said yes."

I have to wait for the whooping and hollering to subside in order to speak again. "How did you know?" I ask them while looking at directly at Marco. He walks over to the phone.

"Hi senorinas. Isn't it great?"

"Hi Marco!! We're so excited. Oh my God, can we go pick out dresses when you get back? We get to wear white too, right? Oh my gosh, we're so excited!!!"

"Me too, girls, me too. I'll explain to your mom about how you knew, ok? You can just catch up now. I'll give you some privacy," he says before walking toward the door.

I give him a look the whole way out. The girls want to talk about the wedding, which I can't help with. I am very pleased that they are so happy. Relieved too. They want to know the details of how he proposed, and all about the beautiful house, and Marco's family. They say they are going to practice their Spanish tomorrow. I miss them and wish they were here. I could use a family squeeze right now.

The call to Nora's is next. I'm not sure how that one is going to go. Less whooping and hollering, I assume.

"Hi, it's me."

Nora speaks loudly to whomever else is in the room, "Sam, Lizzy, it's Nik!" Then to me, "How are you?"

I can tell by the sound of her voice that something is up. "I'm great. How are you guys doing?"

"Great. Anything interesting happening down there?" Yes, there is definitely an odd tone...

I'm not sure I can keep any suspense going.

"Well, yes, actually. Marco proposed. And I said yes."

All I can hear is screaming. I think even Sam is screaming. Lizzy certainly is.

"So, you all knew as well? Was I the only one who didn't know?"

"Will you stop being such a pain and actually enjoy this moment??!!"

"Yes, boss. We're having an amazing time down here. You would not believe how his family lives. It's something out of a romance novel. Seriously."

Lizzy's voice fills the phone next. "Nik, this is the most exciting thing ever! Can you believe both of us are getting married? We could do it in Vegas, together..."

"Hold up there, sweetie. We can work all that out when I get back. And I'm not quite sure I want to encroach on your first and only wedding."

"Ok, bridezillas. Let's not get carried away here."

"You're just jealous," Lizzy says.

"Not really. Not at all, in fact. Sam and I were first, if you remember."

"Now who's the party pooper?!" I hear Lizzy say.

"Hey sweet Nik. I couldn't be happier for you. Maybe you'll trust me next time I tell you you've found a good one." Sam is right, but I can't let him get away with it.

"There will definitely NOT be a next time, Sammy."

"Fair enough, Nik. Fair enough."

"Let's all celebrate when we get back, ok?"

"It's a date. We love you so much Nik!" they all say in unison.

"Love you too. I'll talk to you soon."

The party is still in full force when I go back downstairs. Marco is spinning his nieces around the dance floor, while his sister takes pictures. I just want to stand and watch them, all so beautiful and happy. I can't help but wonder if this is a consequence of all the good news and festivities, or if this is their way of being. I think about staying here, for a long time.

Andres sees me, and pulls me in to dance with him. He is definitely smooth, and knows how to hold a woman. I can see how Marco became the man he is.

"Did you learn to dance like that in America?" he asks as I gracefully execute a spin.

"Yes, sir. My family are all very musical."

"We love to dance in our family, too. Your family now. I hope you will encourage Marco to see us more often. I miss my son very much. At least now I don't have to worry about his heart. It is in good hands, I see."

I smile shakily, afraid I might start to cry. "Andres... I would love to spend more time here. You've all been so wonderful to me. Thank you for welcoming me into your home and your family. I didn't intend to steal all the attention from your celebration!"

"Aaah. This news is much better than an old man getting one year older. Anyhow, tomorrow night will be mine," he says with the smile I recognize from his son. Charmers, those Gonzales men.

I kiss him lightly on both cheeks when the song ends, but a new song begins immediately and someone else's arm is around my waist. Marco's cousin is my next partner.

We all switch partners until only the kids are still standing. To think, this is not even the main event, just a warm-up party. I don't know how I will have the stamina for tomorrow.

I finally get to dance with my new fiancé.

"I'd like to stay here for a long time."

"Where? In Argentina? In my dad's house?"

"Maybe. But what I really meant was in your arms."

"That is their sole purpose now, I believe. To hold you, and love you."

I begin to believe one lifetime won't be enough with this man.

"Take me to bed," I whisper in his ear.

"As you wish."

The night comes in waves of delight. We drift off to sleep while talking, and then wake up and find each other, ready to be taken and taken in.

"Marco, I am so happy. This is all so unbelievable to me. I feel like I'm going to wake up any moment now from this dream and..."

"You've made MY dreams come true."

"I love you so much. I love every single thing about you," I say.

"Tell me," he says, provocatively.

"I love how you're kind and brilliant and strong. I love how you look and smell and taste. I love how you're not scared of how crazy I can be."

"Amor..."

"Let me finish. I love how you love your family, and my family, and me. I love how you treat my girls like princesses and my sisters like queens and Sam like a brother. I love what a great lover you are, and how I feel beautiful when I'm around you. I love that you're honest, even when it's hard. I love how safe I feel in your arms and how much I trust you. I love being in love with you."

"Monique..." he takes a deep sigh. "It is my dream come true to make you happy, to show you everyday how smart and beautiful and sexy you are. I love how you can feel everything, what someone is thinking across the room and the perfect thing to say to make anyone feel better. I love how your hands make magic food that heals the world. I love how you cry at everything, even computer commercials. I love how you cover your tender heart when you're out in the world, but you let it be bare with me, when we are alone. I love how fiercely you love your family, and what an amazing mother you are. I love that you show me your desire, and let me experience mine. Frequently.

I love how every man wishes he was me when you are on my arm. I love how you move your body when you dance, and how you follow when I lead. I love that you show off your superstar legs and wish I could make a mold of your butt that I could always have with me. I love that you pretend you're not ticklish, and how your hands feel on my body. I love your mouth, on my mouth, and on my body.

I love how you hold me, really tightly, when you are feeling pleasure. I love how you purr when you're sleeping. I love how you laugh and how you cry and how you tell me you love me. I love that you let me love you."

We look at each other for a long time. This outpouring of love fills the middle of the night, bracketed by passion and a little bit of sleep.

We drift off and I wake up with my hand on his penis. The gratitude continues, with a slightly different twist.

"I love how you're hard whenever I want you to be."

"I love how you're wet whenever I want you to be."

"I love how it feels when you're inside me."

"I love how it feels inside you."

"I love how you take your time."

"I love how time stops when we're together."

"I love how you know exactly what I need."

"I love how you let me explore your body."

"I love your cock."

This makes Marco laugh. "He REALLY loves you!"

We become too absorbed by the building passion to keep talking.

"Thank you for finding me, Marco."

"Thank you for being, Monique."

Morning comes in small streams of sunlight. A knock on the door confirms the day has started.

"Senor? Your father wanted me to tell you there is a family meeting now. Thank you."

"Thank you, Isabella."

"Family meeting?" I ask.

"Yes. That's my father. He leaves nothing to the moment. We are going to plan the day, and the night. Perfection does not come easily, my dear."

"It does for some people," I say as I give him his good morning kiss.

"Maybe we can stay here and miss the meeting," he suggests.

"No way. I'm not going to be the cause of your absence from the family meeting. I'll keep the bed warm for you."

"Nice try. You, my dear, are now part of this family, and are absolutely expected to be present."

"You're kidding."

"Not even a little bit."

We slip into our dressing gowns and go downstairs to find Andres, Marco's sister and brother-in-law, and his two boys in the sitting room. We are the last ones down. I feel a bit embarrassed.

"Good morning everyone," I say trying to feign cheerfulness.

"Good morning lovebirds," says a voice I do not recognize. A man who looks exactly like Marco appears from the kitchen.

"Sebastian!! When did you arrive?"

"Very late last night. I believe you two had already... retired for the night." He is staring at me intently. "Well, this is the future Mrs. Gonzales, I presume?"

"Hello, Sebastian. It is so nice to finally meet you."

"Yes, I understand why Marco was keeping you hidden, just for himself. Pleasure to meet you," he says as he kisses my cheeks.

This guy is as smooth as cream. Everything I heard about him appears to be true. The word lothario immediately comes to mind. Stunningly good looking, almost too pretty, I can't stop looking at him. He notices.

As does Marco, who takes my hand to sit down on the couch on the other side of the room.

"Papa, did the family meeting need to be so early?"

"Yes. We have much to do today. I know you are intoxicated by love now, but we have an important event, if you remember."

"Of course I remember, Papa. That's why we're all here. For you."

Andres is beginning to remind me of Nora, which means I know how to handle him. "Just tell us what you need us to do, Andres. We are at you service."

"I did not expect you to be so obedient..."

"Sebastian, must you be so rude already?" Marco's question, and the tone of his delivery, shock me.

His sister begins to speak very quickly in Spanish. She does not sound happy, but it puts them all in their places. I've never seen Marco get riled so quickly. It makes me wonder if Sebastian's transgression has really been forgiven.

Andres grabs the reigns from this small distraction, and continues with the complex agenda for the day. Everyone's tasks are well defined, and the day is scheduled to the minute. We disperse to get on to our assignments.

Since I have the fewest obligations, Marco is able to slip me into the kitchen, where I spend the afternoon making Andres my famed chocolate cake. The kitchen is a real dream, even with the staff sneaking looks in every now and then. One particular young man, who has apparently been assisting the chef, is so intrigued by what I'm doing that he offers to help me. We can hardly speak to each other, but choose the world of food to communicate. Marco finds us laughing hysterically at the funny face he has drawn in the spilled flour on the counter.

"Well, it looks like you are doing quite well in here."

"I think the cake is going to be great. Miguel was such a help."

Miguel, acting like he may have crossed some unspoken line, begins to stutter and apologize. Almost bowing as he backs away from Marco.

"It's ok," I say to him. "No problemo. Bueno trabajo."

"Gracias, senora. Gracias."

Marco translates the next stream of Spanish for me: "He thinks you are a very good cook. And he is very happy you will now be coming here more often… now that we are getting married."

"Gracias," I say.

Marco makes his way over to me, and gently rubs his thumb across my cheek, cleaning off a stray smudge of flour.

"I must be very messy right now," I admit.

"Yes, a little bit." A smile rises from the bottom of my heart, as I acknowledge the love in his eyes. "Just the way I like it."

12

THE FIRST SONG

Lalune's lessons were going well. She drank in Avanora's teachings with a newfound thirst for being alive. The darkness and despair that had defined her life until that point dissolved under the beam of her focus. The prospect of happiness fueled her efforts and dampened the fear.

In addition to her daily instructions, Lalune began spending time near the surface observing the land-walkers, to learn their ways and copy their manners. They continued to be as odd as they were enticing. She practiced her singing whenever she could, less afraid of getting caught, and gradually accepting the degree of her desire.

The island, un-inhabited by the land-walkers and regarded as relatively safe by the mermaids, became Lalune's second home. The large ship that had been slowly approaching that area stopped in the path directly between her home and the island. Lalune found it curious that it did not move for several days, but was so absorbed in her own world that she did not think more about it.

Although she could see and hear the land-walkers on the ship clearly, she was fairly certain that her body and voice were hidden from their detection. This strange event was not going to stop keep her from progressing towards her goal.

Something made her listen to them more closely on that cloudy day.

"We are shifting the location of the blasts, due to the oncoming weather system. Not going to take any chances."

Lalune was shocked by what she overheard, and began to study these boat-men carefully. She gleaned that they were planning a series of explosions to look for oil in the ocean that was her home.

She was too scared to warn her family because she should never have been around the land-walkers.

She went back and forth for days, trying to decide what to say, and if she should say anything at all. All of the anxiety about her transformation was dwarfed by the fear for her family, and her community, and she finally realized it was worth their inevitable anger to save their lives.

She decided to go straight to her father. He would know what to do and had the authority to lead the community. Lalune felt the first explosion as she entered his chamber. It was too soon! She thought there would still be days to inform everyone.

The bombing shook their home and sent the mermaids fleeing, hardly getting out in time. The sea creatures scrambled in a frenzy, trying to find safety from the deafening sound and their crumbling seafloor. The whales, the most sensitive, were driven mad by the vibrations, and sped towards the mainland shore.

Lalune knew that the vibrations confused their sense of direction, and they would end up beaching themselves in the shallow water near shore. Panic filled her body, but her instincts led her to follow a pod of whales racing inland. Not knowing what else to do, she began to sing.

She used all the power she could muster to reach them with her voice. Miraculously, they began to slow down, and then change direction. They were regaining their bearings, and swimming toward her. These enormous creatures, the most revered in her world, were drawn enough by her song to stop their fatal drive.

They floated in the calmness of the sea, away from the explosions, and listened to her. As they began to move back into the belly of the ocean, they returned her calls. Lalune trusted that they would now be safe, and their calls would protect any of the others driven mad by the explosions.

As her mighty friends swam away she realized that she had proven her voice could save lives, and could change the course of destruction. Maybe the whales would return and tell everyone her story, how she had saved them. Maybe the mermaids would forgive her her grave transgression. She could only hope.

The swim, trying to keep up with the whales, nearly all the way to the shore of the land-walker's island, left Lalune tired and disoriented. Her second realization came slowly as she recognized where she was - that magical place Avanora had taken her so long ago. Actually, even closer to the mainland but still dense with magic, and as close to the land-walker's home as she had ever been. This was the perfect opportunity to attempt her final move.

Lalune made the decision to complete the rest of the plan that night. She was ready to implement all her knowledge, and test the old mermaid's spells. Perhaps all this chaos and commotion was a sign from the Great Mother that it was time. Either way, Lalune was going to surrender to the opportunity as it lay before her.

The sun was low in the sky and the beach was nearly empty but Lalune had to wait until complete darkness to swim onto the shore and find a rock to block her from view. This was where she would spend her last night as a mermaid.

Lalune began to recite the incantations she had memorized what felt like ages ago, then removed the stone from the scales near her fin and placed it in her mouth without swallowing. This stone had not left her side since Avanora had imbued it with the magic of communication. This was nearly the most important facet of her transformation, she believed.

Lalune hoisted her body onto the sandy ledge of the enormous rock. Everything felt so heavy and clumsy and it filled her with a flash of dread about her future. Would life lose its buoyancy? Did all land-walkers feel this heavy?

The waiting was killing her. Too many thoughts, both positive and negative, consumed her. There was nothing she could do but trust that her decision was the right one.

Lalune did not believe she would be able to sleep but the exhaustion from the day eventually overtook her.

Her instincts opened her eyes as the sun came over the horizon. It was so spectacularly beautiful, she almost forgot what she was doing on shore. As her eyes adjusted to the warm air, and the bright light, she realized her body was now covered in a green silk dress, and where her tail had been was now a set of legs, beautiful legs.

It did not feel any different than her tail from the inside, but stroking her hands down her new skin, free of scales, was a euphoric experience. A wiggle of her toes made her erupt in bubble-filled laughter, which nearly startled her off her precarious position on the rock.

This is what it sounds like to be on land. It is enchanting, like music, all the time.

She laughed even louder, and the buoyancy of her voice brought her to her feet. My goodness, the sand! What a feeling. Gritty and dry, almost dry, a little bit cold and a little bit warm. As if all of the universe was contained in those bits of sand.

Standing up straight was a revelation. The feel of gravity pulling strongly down on her body was unlike anything she had ever experienced. Instead of gliding gracefully, she clunked along like a tentative toddler. I will not fall, she told herself, even though there was no one there to witness it or laugh at her. Just one step after another, she thought.

It took four or five strolls along the shoreline, being careful to miss the water with her toes, until she felt more comfortable on the legs, her legs. Easier than I thought it would be, she thought. Maybe all those exercises the old mermaid taught me were worth it. She felt strong and tingled with excitement.

Lalune heard the sound of voices, deep voices. There were land-walkers coming, more than one. What were they doing here so early? And then she remembered the ones who rode the waves. Yes, they would come out before all the others so that they would have the ocean to themselves. She feared them, as they passed above her family's home on occasion and could have discovered her and her mermaid community. But now she was one of them, and had nothing to fear. What should she do?

Was it odd that she was also there so early? Would they know that she was not like them?

There was only one way to know and only one way to go toward her dream. She would smile and she would sing. Yes, that is it. She did not care if they noticed her or not, but it was time to let her song find ears to land on.

She began very quietly, unsure of how to use her lungs to project sound after a lifetime of being used otherwise. The sound was sweet and soft and otherworldly. She had no words, only soft round vowels, imitating the beguiling sounds of her own language.

The noise of the land-walker males grew closer and closer. They were laughing and speaking loudly. No matter, she could continue singing and wouldn't mind if they paid her any attention or not. But they stopped. Nearly all of them. Perhaps shocked by the appearance of a lone woman on the beach they called their own. The old mermaid had warned her that they would find her irresistible. Was it true? Never mind. It was no concern of hers.

They were looking at her, and she was trying not to look at them. Just taking small steps on her brand new legs and singing her soft sweet song. It made her happy to hear it, regardless of who else was around.

There were five of them, and they were putting on their black water suits and whispering. Perhaps about her. Yes, certainly about her. She smiled.

One of them began to walk toward her, and another followed him.

"Hey, wait for me! I saw her first!"

She understood them, as expected. Now, would she speak and test out her new language? Was it not too soon?

She was nervous. Very nervous. It was bad enough that her legs were a bit wobbly but now she may have to speak. What if the only thing that came out was Mermese? No time to wonder because the first one had reached her.

"Hi," he said. "We heard you singing."

"It was so beautiful," the second one said.

She liked their faces, especially the second one. He did not look at her directly, but hid his face slightly. Was this called embarrassment? The first one just stared, which was closer to what she was expecting.

"We've never seen you here before," the first one said.

"Your singing was so beautiful," repeated number two.

"You already said that, genius," said number one, while his friend turned red.

"Do you surf?" asked number two. What would she say? That she could ride the waves with more grace and strength than anything they could muster? That the ocean had been the only home she had known until this point?

"No, I don't," she said. "I was just taking a... walk... on the beach." The words flowed so beautifully and perfectly. She was doing it!!!

So excited, she let out a little giggle. Number one looked at her quizzically, but the second one, with the nice face that turned red, just smiled. So big that it took up his whole head. He finally held his head up long enough that she could look at it.

"My name is Peter," he said.

"I'm Aaron," said number one.

"My name is Claire." She heard the words come out of her mouth, but did not understand why. She never used her given name. Why didn't she say Lalune?

This was a whole new life and required a whole new name. Clair de la Lune was too much, she guessed, for these land-walkers, but maybe Claire would work.

"That's a beautiful name," beamed number two, now known as Peter.

"Is that all you can say??" asked number one. Although his name was Aaron, all she could think of was arrogant. She wanted him to get out of the way so she could keep looking at Peter.

"We're going surfing now," Peter said. "I guess you don't want to join us."

"No, I can't right now. Do you mind if I just watch?" She did not know where these words were coming from, but she was pleased with them nonetheless.

"Wow, that would be great!! Will you really wait here on the beach for us?"

It would give her time to recall all that Avanora had instructed her, to create this new life. There was a lot to review and plan.

"Yes. Yes, I will."

It was a beautiful day for a song.

*   *   *   *   *   *

GRATITUDES

This book took a hold of me, like a highly skilled lover, and had its way. All my resistance to the process – so foreign for a spiritual essay writer – was no match for the intensity of desire and passion that filled me.

Like any fine ravaging, it took many hands.

Thank you Chela Davison for the vision that birthed the two primary characters and Graciela (Mamita) Masso for the cover inspiration. Profound appreciation and awe to the A-team (Bibi, Alex, Sarah, Kurt, Heather, Marianne, Renee, Lori, Allison, Carole, Cil), who read terrible drafts, over and over again. And still spoke to me in the morning.

Deepest thanks to the lovers who demonstrated how healing great sex can be, (you know who you are), the Muse whose light spankings I rather enjoyed, and the magical Universe that keeps feeding me blessings, lessons and fairy tales… in flesh and blood.

ABOUT THE AUTHOR

Pascale Kavanagh believes that life is magically delicious. The twists and turns of her full life, from NY dancer to MIT engineer to Global Spiritual Teacher, have provided an arsenal of stories and lessons about fierce compassion, intrepid self-inquiry, and the practice of satisfaction.

This sad shy girl turned bold soul regularly waves her magic wand to turn suffering into grace and joy. As an inspirational teacher, speaker and writer, her words capture the essence of miracles.

Pascale's work can be found throughout the internet, in corporate board rooms, on exotic beaches, and an occasional African safari.

When not rocking the stage and the page, Pascale can be found *feeding her soul* by loving her little mermaid to excess, globe-trotting to the next great adventure, and sporting bright red lips as a tango diva.

You can find Pascale's guidance on the sacred art of satisfaction at www.feedyoursoul.com, a portal for love, laughs and maybe even a sexy story or two.